1 - 49 $\frac{30}{20}$

SOMETHING FUNNY

By the same author

A TEMPORARY AFFAIR

SOMETHING FUNNY

Imogen Parker

HAMISH HAMILTON · LONDON

HAMISH HAMILTON LTD

Published by the Penguin Group
Penguin Books Ltd, 27 Wrights Lane, London w8 5tz, England
Penguin Books USA Inc., 375 Hudson Street, New York, New York 10014, USA
Penguin Books Australia Ltd, Ringwood, Victoria, Australia
Penguin Books Canada Ltd, 10 Alcorn Avenue, Toronto, Ontario, Canada m4v 3b2
Penguin Books (NZ) Ltd, 182–190 Wairau Road, Auckland 10, New Zealand

Penguin Books Ltd, Registered Offices: Harmondsworth, Middlesex, England

First published 1995
1 3 5 7 9 10 8 6 4 2

Copyright © Imogen Parker, 1995

The moral right of the author has been asserted

Typeset by Datix International Limited, Bungay, Suffolk
Printed in Great Britain by Clays Ltd, St Ives plc
Filmset in 11.5/14.5pt Monophoto Baskerville

A CIP catalogue record for this book is available from the British Library

ISBN 0–241–13563-X

Acknowledgements

I am grateful to Ariel Bruce and Dave Laws for their advice, and to Becky Parker and Nicholas Duggan for their unwavering support.

For the Nellists.

Prologue

I had finally made it to Paris. City of art, philosophy, love. But this was mid-December, and as I trudged through the slushy gutters of the Boulevard St-Germain, it seemed about as romantic as Camden High Street on a rainy night. All the immaculately attired Parisian Christmas shoppers were walking determinedly in the opposite direction. I wondered how it was that smart people never felt the cold, and why they never stepped on the bit of snow that turned out to be a deep puddle collecting over a blocked drain.

The café Le Mandarin was a welcoming sight. Warm gold light from the low-slung, lace-shaded lanterns creating clear portholes in the steam-fogged windows. I pushed open the door and looked around.

There were a few tables occupied by married men and their mistresses, or so I imagined, because of the very public exchanges of patisserie and saliva. No wonder there were so many food shops in Paris. The male population led a culinary double life, eating a full day's calories with their mistresses before, presumably, going home to *coq au vin* with their wives.

The waiter appeared distressed that I was dripping on his floor and tried to show me to a back table where I wouldn't be visible from the street. After just a few days in Paris, I was used to this tactic. I pretended I couldn't understand him, and plonked myself resolutely in one of the booths at the front, without even bothering to take off my duffle coat.

I asked for a *café crème* and waited for Charlotte.

She had obviously been in Paris for some time because she had the look of a native: short black fringeless bob waxed back over her scalp and behind her ears, pale face (instinctively I touched my nose and knew that it was red as a clown's from the cold), mulberry lips. She was wearing black, as she'd said she would: a black swing coat, black leggings, expensive, unsplashed black ankle-boots and gloves – the only sign of frivolity – made of fake leopardskin. Not my idea of a student at the Sorbonne. I tried to slip out of my duffle coat and managed to knock a teaspoon off the table in the process. It clattered, like a canteen of cutlery, to the floor, and made her look in my direction. I waved feebly.

We introduced ourselves formally. She beckoned the waiter over and ordered a tisane. Then she said, 'Right, why don't you explain why you're here?'

So I started to tell her the story.

Chapter One

I'm not really someone who believes in omens, fate, that sort of thing, but when I discovered on the first day of working at the bank that my predecessor, whose swivel chair I was sitting in, had been murdered, I didn't feel it was an auspicious beginning.

The day had already got off to a bad start when I was physically prevented from taking the lift to the sixth floor by a man in a quasi-military uniform. My boss, who was new to the bank too, hadn't realized that he needed to inform security about my arrival. I spent a good half-hour sitting in one of the low leather armchairs next to the fountain while the grumpy receptionist endeavoured to contact Martin. Eventually, I got up and took a walk around the huge central atrium, pausing to look over the circular balustrade at the centre down into an indigo pool below. A woman wearing a black swimming costume and goggles was swimming energetic lengths which began and ended out of my line of sight. The receptionist watched me suspiciously, as if I were about to drop litter down the well, and called the guard over for a whispered consultation. My joke about his security firm, which had recently been criticized in the press for failing to detect guns being smuggled into a prison, didn't help matters along, and it was only when Martin arrived, apologizing profusely for having been delayed by a bomb scare at Waterloo, that I was allowed to penetrate the building.

The lifts that I had been watching as I sat in the sumptuous palm-fringed reception area were like adjustable glass lanterns sliding noiselessly up and down the interior walls of the building.

'Pretty snazzy, hey?' said Martin.

'Amazing,' I replied, as I watched the little green landscape fall away from us.

'The building's virtually empty, apart from our four floors, and there's a health club sort of thing in the basement. Sorry about being late on your first day.'

'That's OK. I didn't quite realize that the recession had hit places like this too,' I said as we glided past floor after floor of unused office space.

'Where have you been? Loads of developers have gone bust. You can get offices like this dirt cheap these days. Here we are,' he added, as a soft bell pinged and the doors opened on to a carpeted corridor. I had to run to keep up with his fast pace. He paused in front of a polished walnut-panelled door, which seemed out of place in such high-tech surroundings, and patted his smart suit jacket, frisking himself for his wallet.

'Listen, Martin, I don't think it's a good idea to be so familiar with me in public,' I said.

'Ooh, Miss Fitt, what are you suggesting?' he replied, putting on a silly voice.

'Here it is. Phew!' He pulled the wallet from his back trouser pocket with a sigh of relief.

'I'm serious, Martin. While I'm in this building, I'm your secretary, not your friend. You know how people are. They'll start gossiping and it won't be good for your authority.'

'So what am I meant to do, ignore you?'

'No, but I just don't think it was very smart to rush up

to me screaming "*Sorry*, Soph!" and hugging me like you just did in reception.'

'Point taken,' said Martin. He took out a credit-card-sized identity key and swiped it through a panel at the side. The door clicked open.

'I'll get you one of these,' he said, holding the door open for me.

After the relative tranquillity of the central atrium, the noise from the dealing room nearly knocked me over. The markets were already open and there was a lot of shouting and gesticulating. A couple of blokes turned to see who was coming in and wolf-whistled at me as I stepped over the threshold. They immediately fell silent when they saw that I was closely followed by their boss. Martin seemed unperturbed as he led me to his office, past the banks of dealers, offering a curt 'Good-morning' to those who weren't on the phone.

He showed me to my office, which was really just a desk with three drawers, a computer terminal, keyboard and printer in a little anteroom between Martin's office and the dealing room. It had smoked-glass walls, which enabled me to see out rather better than others could see in. There was, to my enormous relief, a door to shut out some of the noise.

There was a memo on my desk from someone called Marie, computer controller, giving me my pass code for the computer. I switched it on and stared at the screen. It was a system I was reasonably familiar with. There were a few messages for Martin which I printed out and put on his ridiculously large mock-Victorian desk.

I watched Martin conferring with one of the dealers on the Deutschmark desk and was rather surprised to notice

5

that the dealer, who was not a lot younger than Martin himself, flinched at one of his instructions and then nodded vigorously, trying hard to please. Martin wandered around the dealing room, listening in to some of the calls, exchanging information with the twenty or so dealers, and generally being in charge. The new job obviously suited him and he seemed to have grown in confidence in the two years since I last worked with him. As I watched him prowling around being boss, I felt an almost maternal sense of pride.

I had known Martin many years. We met at the American bank where we both began our careers. We had become friends on the first day, partly because we seemed to be the only graduate recruits who had a healthy disrespect for our chosen profession. My disrespect, however, turned out to have more stamina than Martin's, because one day, after five years on the corporate side of the bank, I decided to give up the whole career rat race in favour of finding out what I really wanted to do with my life.

I had spent the time since then temping during the week and doing a stand-up comedy routine most weekends in various north London pubs, hoping that one day a new life would miraculously reveal itself to me. It hadn't. Although my jobs varied all the time, I eventually began to feel that I was stagnating in a routine almost as oppressive as my career had become, and one that was far less well paid. So I decided to travel for a while, equipped myself with a qualification to teach English as a Foreign Language so that I could work abroad if I needed to, and was on the point of leaving England indefinitely and renting out my flat to tenants.

Costas, the freeholder of the flats in my building, had chosen that moment to inform me that we had subsidence, and my share of the insurance excess, payable immediately so that the underpinning work could be started, was £2,000. That accounted for all the money I had managed to save, and a little bit more.

As my fortunes fell, Martin's had risen. He had just been head-hunted to manage the foreign-exchange dealing room of a rival bank. In the way of these things, the old bank marched him out the moment he proffered his notice and the new bank wanted him to start immediately. I could tell he was nervous about the new job when we met for a quick sandwich lunch on his first day. There was much more responsibility than he was used to and there seemed to be quite a lot of bad feeling among the dealers about his appointment.

. He needed an assistant he could trust, but where was he going to find one at such short notice, he asked me, wiping a blob of egg mayonnaise from his nose.

I began to list the more efficient temps I had encountered.

'You wouldn't consider the job yourself, Soph?' he interrupted.

'Me? Work for you?' I cried. 'No way!'

'Well, why not? You need the money. I need someone who knows their way around. I get the impression that it's not the happiest place.'

'Oh, now you're really tempting me . . .' I said.

'Come on, you've worked in difficult environments before. Go on, Soph, help me out. It might be fun.'

'No. I couldn't work in a bank again, and, anyway, it would ruin our friendship.'

'Course it wouldn't. Come on. Just for a couple of months?' he wheedled.

'No.'

'Please . . . I'll pay you fifty per cent more than your normal rate. And you wouldn't have to pay agency fees. How about that?'

'Oh, all right then,' I said.

'Honestly, Soph, I don't know why you ever left banking. You drive a pretty hard bargain,' said Martin ruefully.

Martin finished his tour of the dealing room and went straight into a meeting with another soberly dressed man whose office, a mirror-image of Martin's, was situated in the opposite corner of the dealing floor. I was musing about the sartorial hierarchy at the bank. My initial impression was that the more senior the staff, the duller their ties, which led me on to the observation that there were only two women in the room – myself and the secretary sitting in the anteroom to the office, where I could see Martin talking.

My phone rang.

'Den?' said a male voice.

'No, I'm sorry, it's Sophie. Can I help?'

'Oh. Sorry,' said the voice and rang off.

I put down the receiver. It rang again almost immediately. I said hallo but there was no reply.

I made a mental note to ask Martin how he wanted me to answer his phone, thinking that I was going to find it difficult to refer to myself as Martin Young's secretary with the appropriate degree of deference. I looked at my screen again, checking for messages. There were none. I was beginning to get bored. There wasn't a lot of activity now on the dealing-room floor. The expected interest-rate cut had failed to materialize and the markets were settling down after the early morning's activity. The Reuters screen above the door repeated the same news it had been showing for the past hour. Below it were three digital displays registering the dollar, Deutschmark and yen rates, which were virtually unfluctuating now, and below them a bank of clock faces showing the time in New York, Japan and Hong Kong. The hours before lunch (or breakfast, tea and dinner in those cities) seemed to be moving exceptionally slowly.

I was dying for a cup of coffee and, since nobody seemed to be falling over themselves to show me around, I decided to explore. Just as I was leaving my office the phone rang again.

'Den, is that you?'

'This is Mr Young's office,' I replied, stifling a chuckle. 'Who's calling?'

The receiver at the other end of the line was replaced with a click.

I called the switchboard and found myself talking to the grumpy receptionist I had encountered earlier. I told her that I had received two calls for somebody called Den.

'Well, what am I supposed to do about it? He asked for your extension,' she said accusingly and cut me off.

I found the small kitchen relatively easily. There was a handwritten sign above the coffee machine which said, 'If you take the final cup, just be sure you fill it up!!!'

I have an aversion to officious little notices that pretend to be amusing, especially if they contain rhymes or exclamation marks, so I was glad to see that it had been ignored and the coffee jug was empty. I threw the used cone filter away, found some new ones in the cupboard, as well as some poor-quality ground coffee which was labelled 'office use!', filled the machine with water and switched it on. I discovered that the other cupboards were bare except for some sachets of hot chocolate, each labelled 'Pat's'. Apart from a few pints of milk and a couple of yoghurts, also labelled, that had passed their sell-by date, the fridge was empty too.

One of the junior dealers (I guessed his status from his pink tie with large yellow spots) poked his head round the door and said with a wink, 'Mine's black with two sugars, love.'

'Shall we try that again?' I asked. 'It goes, hallo, you're new here, aren't you? What's your name? Well, Sophie, welcome aboard. Is that coffee you're making? Well, if it's not too much trouble, could I have a cup when it's ready? . . . Then you tell me your name, you see? It's quite easy.' Somehow what was meant to be light banter came out rather pompously.

'Oh, forget it,' said the dealer and walked off.

I later heard him whispering to one of his colleagues, 'Steer clear, mate. I think she's a fucking feminist or something.'

As I was pouring out a cup of coffee for myself, the woman I had seen sitting in the other office walked in.

'What a morning!' she said. 'I was in at eight-thirty and this is the first chance I've had for a breather. Mr Young tells me you're called Sophie. I'm Pat.'

After two years more or less constant temping you get to recognize certain office types and I immediately spotted Pat as the office martyr. She was middle-aged and slightly overweight – the sort of person who is always eating biscuits but never enjoying them because she is meant to be dieting. I would have bet money that she was rushed off her feet but that she made coffee for all the dealers as well as her boss, and washed up all their dirty cups too, sighing all the while, but not letting anyone help.

'I'd better take three cups,' she said. 'Mr Young'll be parched by now too.'

If there was a note that implied criticism in her voice, I chose to ignore it.

She poured out two large mugs and found that there was hardly any coffee left.

'Oh, well, I'll just have a mouthful,' she said. 'Soon be lunch after all.'

'I'll make some more for Mart . . . Mr Young,' I offered.

'Oh, no, don't worry. I'd better be getting back. By the way, if there's anything you need to know . . .' She was out of the door before I could respond.

'Where can I find Den?' I asked her disappearing back.

She stopped in her tracks and turned round.

'Oh. Didn't anyone tell you?'

'No. What?'

'Why should they really? I'd have thought you'd have seen it in the papers, though,' she went on mysteriously.

'What?' I asked.

'Denise is in a better place.'

As she said it her voice cracked, and I realized she wasn't referring to a more lucrative job. Pat pulled a hanky from the cuff of her cardigan and dabbed at her eyes.

'She was attacked on the Northern Line near Tooting. It was one of those people who'd been let out of a mental hospital, you know. What a waste! She was a lovely girl. Very lively.' Her voice trailed off in reflection. 'A bit too lively for some, if you know what I mean, but she had a lot of courage.' Pat was now warming to her theme. 'She put up quite a struggle. Funnily enough, she'd been doing a self-defence course at the club downstairs. The police said that's what killed her. If she'd been calm, they wouldn't have used the knife. But she wasn't like that. She wouldn't be told. Oh, no, not our Denise . . .'

The last few phrases spoke volumes to me about the late Denise's relationship with Pat. It sounded as if there had been a power struggle of some sort. I felt that Pat wasn't entirely unhappy that Denise was no longer around.

I felt myself trembling.

'And she used to sit in my office?' I asked.

'Yes. I think somebody should have told you really.'

'Yeah. So do I,' I said.

Martin wasn't around for the rest of the day. While I was making coffee he had left a note on my desk saying, 'Get Pat to show you round. Be back late p.m. Drink?' I was half inclined to walk out of the job there and then, but I decided that I wanted to give Martin a piece of my mind for failing to tell me about the murder. He, of all people, must have known that I wouldn't have agreed to take the job if I had known about the circumstances. I felt as if I had been conned by my best friend.

There was nothing for me to do since I fully intended to quit. My attempt at badinage with the man in the kitchen had not made me any friends among the dealers, who studiously ignored me. I sat in my glass office feeling like a lone goldfish in a bowl on the sideboard.

At lunchtime, Pat rang me up to say that she was just too busy to have lunch out, but there was a good sandwich bar over the road, and while I was there, would I mind getting her two rounds of cream cheese and date on white – she shouldn't really, but it was one of those days.

*

Outside, it was a beautiful warm summer's day. I felt my body relax and open to the sun, absorbing the heat gratefully after the chill of the office air-conditioning. I was wearing only a flimsy forties-style crêpe dress, and I had been shivering all morning.

I found a little café on a side street with a couple of tables outside and I sat in a cloud of diesel fumes, eating my salt beef on rye.

Have you ever noticed that at the slightest hint of a fine day Londoners dust off their garden furniture and sit outside amid the traffic noise and pollution, pretending that they are in a sun-dappled Mediterranean piazza, and that narrow British pavements can sustain a café culture as well as any foreign boulevard?

I was tipping my face back to catch the last few rays of ultraviolet before the sun disappeared behind a copper-coloured mirror-glass tower, when a loud London voice said, 'D'you mind if I sit here?'

Under my sunglasses, I opened an eye.

'Sure,' I said, indicating that the very tall, slim woman who had asked the question could share my table.

'Thanks.'

From over her shoulder she swung a heavy transparent-plastic duffle bag that seemed to be full of cosmetic bottles. A pink and green striped towel spilled out of the top. She plonked the bag down beside her, then went to pick up her tray of food.

I watched amazed as she proceeded to demolish two salt-beef sandwiches, a tub of coleslaw, six gherkins and an oily-looking piece of coconut cake.

I finished my bottle of mineral water and stood up. Before I left I couldn't help asking, 'Would you mind telling me how you keep so thin if you eat like that?'

She let out a loud, raucous laugh.

13

'I've got a fast metabolism and I do a lot of exercise, but do you know what uses up most calories?'

I shook my head.

'Sex,' she said. 'I'm not joking. You can forget about high fibre and low sodium and all that crap if you're having a regular bonk.'

I caught a glimpse of myself in the washroom mirror later on that afternoon. It's not that I'm fat, but when you're five foot two, any extra pound shows. Sex, I thought. I'm obviously not getting enough of it.

We drank a rather sombre bottle of New Zealand Sauvignon while Martin persuaded me that he hadn't known about Denise's demise either. He was quite upset by the news, feeling, as I had, that he had been lied to by default. He said he had been told at his interview that there was an experienced secretary in place, but when he started work he had been told by the vice-president he reported to that she had left.

'I think his precise words were, "Denise is no longer with us",' he remembered. 'But then he said something like, "That's quite convenient for you", because it meant that I could get off to a clean start. What a bastard!'

'So you had no idea?' I said. 'Oh, Martin, I'm sorry I shouted at you. I just thought . . .'

'That's OK. Really. I do understand. But you won't leave, will you?'

'Well, it kind of freaks me out, you know.'

'Just stay till I find someone else.'

'All right then,' I said reluctantly.

'Shall we have another bottle?' Martin asked, as he emptied the last drops of Cloudy Bay into my glass.

We were sitting in a dingy basement wine bar over the

road from the bank. It smelt musty, like the inside of an empty sherry barrel.

'I don't think so,' I said.

A gloom had descended on both of us. Martin offered me a ten-pound note to get a taxi home. Normally I would be too proud to accept hand-outs, but since I was broke and I didn't fancy the tube, I took it.

It was still light outside and the air felt balmy. Martin hailed a taxi and hugged me affectionately before I got in.

'See you tomorrow, then,' he said.

I pulled down the window as the taxi executed a U-turn and saw that Pat was just leaving the bank, her head down, pretending not to have witnessed our parting.

Chapter Two

The first phone call I received the next morning was a hang-up. The second was from my mother, telling me that Reg had suffered a mild heart attack during the night and was in Northwick Park Hospital. There was nothing I could do. She would let me know when I could visit. In the meantime, I wasn't to worry.

I spent the entire morning in a state of anxiety, since Mum always tries to protect me from bad news and I didn't believe that the situation was as under control as she was insisting. My mother is always calm in a crisis – one of the many characteristics I do not share with her.

In a brief gap between his constant meetings, Martin sensibly suggested that I ring the hospital, and I spoke to a doctor who assured me that Reg was comfortable but a bit tired. He said that I could visit the next evening. I felt a bit better after talking to him.

Martin was giving a contingent of Japanese from the Tokyo branch of the bank a guided tour. He asked me to find a Japanese restaurant with a large enough table for them all to have lunch. I set up a restaurant file on the computer, giving the name, address and telephone number of each place and intending to add a brief review as Martin reported back, awarding stars for service, speed, atmosphere, food and price (which seemed to have become an important factor in the years since I had been the proud and profligate owner of a company credit card). It was taking secretarial efficiency to extremes, but since Martin had been too busy to give me any other work, I had nothing else to do. I found myself wondering whether, if I stayed long enough, I could produce a guide to City restaurants and sell it to other banks and businessmen.

Imagining trays of luscious sushi, pickled ginger and thimbles-full of warm sake all morning had ruined my appetite for a granary bap, so I decided to investigate the health club in the basement of the building. There was an advert in the washroom, strategically Sellotaped next to the full-length mirror, saying that there was a special offer. Employees of the bank were entitled to one month's free membership. I suspected that this concession would not apply to a temp, but I didn't intend to tell them that I was a temp. The identity card that had been sitting on my desk when I arrived that morning gave my name, but no indication of my status.

There were at least ten reasons to hate the girl on the front desk (long, glossy chestnut hair that didn't stick to her designer sweatshirt, thighs that looked really good in cycling shorts, that kind of thing), but as well as being alarmingly beautiful, she seemed very nice and helpful. Handing me a large white towel with the club's green-apple logo embroidered in one corner, she informed me that all the personal trainers were busy at the moment but I was welcome to have a look around and take a complimentary sauna if I fancied one.

I walked quickly past the studios where classes of martial arts and step-aerobics were in progress and through the gym, which was mirrored, making it look as if the rows of state-of-the-art weights machines stretched to infinity. The centrepiece of the club was a large rectangular swimming pool, the middle of which I had been looking into the morning before. It was surrounded by an arcade of white columns beneath which a buffet-style restaurant had been created, with dark-green garden tables and chairs. There were palm trees and pots of geraniums and the whole area was dripping with ivy, which I couldn't resist pinching to see if it was real. The space had the humid, slightly composty smell of a greenhouse and I wondered how they managed to keep the plants looking so healthy with so little natural light. A parakeet in a cage squawked behind me, making me jump. I hoped that the club, which was called Eden, didn't extend its theme to live snakes.

The ladies' changing room, or Eve's Place, as it said on the door, was a fantasy grotto for the vain and body-conscious. The warren of little rooms, each housing a different treat, was like a subterranean cave. The Jacuzzi would comfortably seat six, the sauna was fragrant with eucalyptus. There was a whole complex of steam rooms with a plunge pool at the end. A door from the shower and locker area led to the therapy rooms, which I didn't bother to investigate after a quick glance at the price list.

There was half an hour remaining of my lunch break. I deliberated for a few seconds over whether to sauna or to eat. Vowing to bring in my swimming costume the next day, to make all that undressing and dressing worth-while, I headed to the restaurant area. There was a small selection of colourful salads, a range of interesting breads and a tureen of chilled tomato and basil soup. I ladled out a bowl of that and took a piece of ciabatta studded with black olives. I couldn't see where I was supposed to pay and I was standing holding my tray, trying to spot a till and a free table, when a voice behind me said, 'Hi again!'

It took me a few seconds to place the face. I found

myself looking at her tray for inspiration. It was loaded with several pieces of bread, a large mixed salad and two of the rich-looking desserts that the menu, chalked up on a blackboard, referred to as Sins.

'Oh, hallo!' I said, my brain finally making the connection with the woman from the sandwich bar the day before.

'Oh, look, they're moving.' She pointed at a table near the pool. 'Shall we share a table?'

'Good idea,' I replied.

'Ally Capellino, isn't it?' she said, as we sat down.

'No, Sophie Fitt,' I said, joking. 'Oh, you meant my jacket.' It was a short caramel cashmere jacket with a brown velvet collar and pocket flaps. I hung it over the back of my chair. 'It's a bit warm for this weather,' I continued, 'but it's like sitting in a fridge upstairs with the air-conditioning.'

'I had a skirt of hers last year, but it was such good-quality wool, it was caviare to moths,' she replied. 'Jools, by the way.' She spoke quickly, with a strong London accent. 'What's upstairs, then?'

'Upstairs, or uplift, I suppose I should say, since there doesn't seem to be anything as low-tech as a staircase in this building, is the bank where I'm working. Where do you work?'

'All over the place, really,' she said. 'I'm a model. Don't look so surprised. I look better with make-up on.'

I said that I was only looking surprised because models were pretty thin on the ground in the City. She said that as a matter of fact they quite often used the modern architecture of the Lloyd's building as a backdrop to fashion shoots, but I probably looked at the clothes and not the surroundings, which was the whole point.

'We're doing a catalogue for the autumn/winter season down by Billingsgate. Typical. I'm prancing up and down in winter clothes in the middle of a bloody heatwave.'

Her hair was still wet from showering. It was short at the back and was combed severely away from her face. As it began to dry, the colour lightened to a rich auburn and the fringe fell forward, softening her striking, angular features. She said she was twenty-two and it was increas-ingly difficult to get work because of her age.

'I'm not kidding, they're all sixteen and seventeen now. Anyway, now you know all about me. What about you?'

When I first became a temp I very soon discovered that going to Cambridge, then getting a highly paid executive job in an American bank, then giving it up on a whim, was not a life story designed to make me many friends among my new colleagues. But I didn't feel the need to be discreet with Jools, since she didn't work for the bank and she was so straightforward herself, and she asked such direct questions that I found myself opening up, giving her a potted life history, even mentioning my stand-up comedy routine.

We seemed to get on instantly. I liked her no-nonsense way of talking and her abandoned laugh. From her unflattering descriptions of the other models who were involved in the catalogue, I imagined she was feeling as lonely in her new job as I was.

It's my experience that however short a contract is, one of the first things you have to do on a new job is to find your best-friend-at-work. Normally it's someone in the office you can have a giggle with, or someone you trust enough to let off steam with down the pub on

Friday night. A kind of safety valve. It didn't look as if that person was going to emerge on the sixth floor of the building, so I was delighted when Jools said she thought she'd be around for a few more weeks and that she'd call me the next time she was in the gym to see if I was free for lunch.

I walked through the dealing room feeling much happier and I even managed to elicit a smile from the dollar dealer. As I approached my office, I noticed that the trader from the yen desk, with the pink and yellow tie, who was today sporting a pink and white striped shirt, was trying to open the bottom drawer of my desk.

'Hi,' I said to his back.

He straightened up quickly and moved out of the way.

'Looking for a new biro,' he said. 'Mine's run out.'

'Oh. Did Denise keep a supply?'

'Yeah,' he said. 'Not to worry.'

'I'll get you one from the stationery cupboard, if you like,' I said, as a kind of peace offering.

'Don't worry about it. I'll borrow one,' he replied, adding 'thanks' as a reluctant afterthought.

There was no sign of Martin. Since he had said just before leaving at midday that he would be back at two o'clock sharp, I was a little bit cross when he didn't turn up until five.

'Jesus, Martin!' I said as he leant over my shoulder, breathing whisky fumes all over me.

'Productive afternoon?' he asked, stumbling over the words.

'I've been jotting down a few ideas for Saturday, since I had nothing better to do.'

I often find useful material for my stand-up routine

when I start a job. I had just been thinking about the bank and wondering what my characters would make of it.

In my act I usually do monologues by three of the characters I have created. At the moment my favourites are Charity Ball, a very earnest Sloane who cannot do anything remotely enjoyable like having a party without trying to raise money for Riding for the Disabled, or some other good cause; Joy Riding, a bit of a slag who likes unreconstructed macho men; and, undoubtedly the most successful character I have yet created, Something Funny, after whom my moderately successful one-woman show at Edinburgh was named.

She is a middle-aged woman who sees conspiracy at every opportunity and is never happier than when talking about illness, preferably terminal. Her refrain is 'There's something funny going on here.' I really don't know where she came from, but you can hear women like her if you stand at London bus stops for any length of time.

Martin was trying to read the page where I had written:

STRANGER: *These lifts are amazing, aren't they?*
SOMETHING FUNNY: *I can't look. I get vertigo.*
STRANGER: *Beautiful weather we're having.*
SF: *They say it gives you cancer.*
STRANGER: *Really?*
SF: *There's something funny going on with the ozone layer.*
STRANGER: *Well, I expect you're glad of the air-conditioning.*
SF: *It's too cold for me. Gives you legionnaires' disease, apparently.*

'No, it doesn't,' said Martin, slurring the 's'.

'I know that,' I said, sighing.

I went to make him some coffee.

'Is it really wise to get pissed when you're in charge?'

'Pissed? *Moi?* You should have seen the Nips, Soph. One of them passed out in his miso soup.'

'You'd better watch it, you know. Pat told me this morning that your predecessor got the sack for drinking. Did you know that?'

'Nah. Wasn't that,' said Martin.

'What was it, then?'

'Can't tell you, Soph, I'm afraid. Confidentiality.' It took several attempts to get the word out correctly.

'Oh, for heaven's sake!' I said, impatient with him.

He giggled and put a finger to his lips.

'You can huff and puff as much as you like, but my lips are sealed.'

'Oh, grow up!' I said and went back to my notes.

I arrived home feeling somewhat out of sorts. There were no messages on the answerphone, which didn't improve things. I rang Mum to ask about Reg, but she was obviously at the hospital because there was no reply. It was still light, so I poured myself a glass of white wine and went to sit on my roof terrace and analyse why I was feeling so irritable.

It was a summer's evening and as the light faded I could hear birds singing – one of the best features, I think, of an English summer. It's not as good a sound as the chirruping of crickets that emerges after dark in Mediterranean countries, but it is pleasantly evocative of something: childhood perhaps, lying in bed when it's still light with conversation floating up from neighbours' gardens, along with the heavy perfume of phlox and tobacco plants. I used to twist and turn under my cotton sheet, not able to sleep, and wanting to be with the grown-ups. Whenever the weather permitted, Mum and Reg would spend evenings swinging in a yellow and white striped garden chair on the patio outside the french doors, just below my bedroom window. I can still hear the murmur of their chat at the end of the day, and the cracking of ice-cubes in tall glasses as their gin and tonics grew slowly warm, and I can still feel the sense of frustration, because I wasn't tired at all, at not being allowed to join them, which was gently lulled by the birdsong from the copper beech at the end of the garden, until I drifted into sleep.

My calming memory was shattered by a shout of 'I'm leaving, you bastard' from a woman's voice downstairs.

A door slammed, then a man's voice said, 'Bloody well leave, then, you bitch!'

I peered over the railing at the edge of my terrace. I live on the top floor of a four-storey Victorian terraced house in Primrose Hill. At street level there's a launderette and in between it and me there are two recently renovated flats.

One flat was empty and for sale. That's how we found out about the subsidence. Costas, who owns the launderette and the freehold of the entire building, had a buyer for the flat below mine, but their surveyor's report said that the whole terrace was gradually sinking, which put them off.

The other flat, on the first floor, was rented to a couple who had only recently moved in. I hadn't yet met them, since we seemed to keep different hours – with this new job at the bank, I had to be an early riser and their curtains were always drawn when I left the building – but I had heard them arguing several times already. She was always threatening to leave, and he didn't seem to care. It didn't get much worse than that, and since we were having an unusually hot summer and I always had my windows open at night, I would also hear their elaborate and extremely verbal lovemaking sessions later on. In fact I felt I knew their intimacies so well, I wouldn't be able to stop myself blushing if we were ever to meet on the stairs.

'I'm leaving you, you bastard,' she shrieked again.

'Bloody well leave then,' he said.

The door slammed.

Oh, the joys of being single!

I wasn't able to convince myself for very long. It had been ages since I had had a relationship, and I was fed up. At twenty-eight, surely I was meant to be reaching my sexual prime, not sitting on my roof terrace on a perfect summer's evening with only a bottle of Sainsbury's Soave for company?

Before I heard about the subsidence, my plans to go abroad had taken up so much of my time, since I was studying during the day and working shifts in a pizza restaurant in the evening, that I hadn't really noticed that I didn't have a relationship.

I had, for the first time since I was a child, been in touch with my father, who was living in Paris, and my idea had been to meet him *en route* to my new life in Spain or Italy.

Tracking him down had been a major undertaking because he had moved several times since the last address I had for him. Talking on the phone to various people who had sighted him had improved my French but drained my emotional reserves.

When I eventually found him, his response to me had been cautious, if not downright off-putting. If he had known me better (or at all) he would have realized that a challenge makes me very tenacious (my mother calls it contrary) and if he didn't want to see me he would have been far better off issuing a gushing welcome.

I had called him recently to tell him that my plans had changed, and he expressed neither relief nor dismay, which made me feel rather wobbly. It was as if he were completely indifferent to me, which was somehow worse than either a positive or a negative reaction.

Sometimes the anger I felt at being rejected by him all my life welled up inside me and came out in floods of tears sobbed into my pillow at night. Other times, it made me fearsomely determined to prove myself. But recently, I found, I felt just vaguely fed up and tetchy.

'I'm leaving, you bastard,' growled the woman downstairs.

'Oh, bloody well go, then, you stupid fucking prima donna,' I muttered to myself, draining my glass.

I decided to indulge myself by emptying the entire contents of my aromatherapy oil starter pack into a hot bath, where I wallowed for a long time and sang along at top volume to Roy Orbison's *Greatest Hits*.

Chapter Three

'Mwaa, Mwaa!' Mars Tonic, the man who had come to my one-woman show on the Fringe and subsequently asked to be my agent, greeted me rapturously as I walked towards the bar. 'Sophie, sit down here and say hallo to someone terribly important.'

I had met Mars several times in similar circumstances. He was embarrassingly over the top, and I was never 100 per cent sure whether the characters he introduced me to were really independent television producers, as he claimed, or just friends of his who played a role in exchange for a few drinks at the Groucho.

I had been sceptical about receiving a fan letter from an agent, especially one with such a ludicrous name. I thought it must be a practical joke played on me by someone who had been reading too much David Lodge, but when I asked around some of my relatively successful acting friends, I discovered that although Mars had a slightly dodgy reputation his clients often seemed to be in work.

'Some of my protégés are so bloody alternative, even they don't know who they are,' Mars had replied cheerily to my tentative inquiries about his list when I first met him, so I took the hint and decided not to press him further.

I never really knew whether I had become one of Mars's clients or not, but once every couple of months he would ring me and invite me out for a drink with some people he thought I ought to meet, and I would float off after a couple of bottles of champagne feeling very pleased with myself for securing a part in a new television series that was about to be commissioned.

The next morning, swimming around in one of those slightly hallucinatory hangovers too much champagne on an empty stomach inevitably ushers in, I would wonder whether I had imagined the whole evening. After a couple of weeks of hearing nothing, I would be certain I had.

Still, Mars was good company, and I've never been known to turn down free champagne. This evening, however, I had decided to be abstemious. I had promised to visit Reg in hospital, and visiting hours ended at nine o'clock. I calculated that one quick drink, a taxi to Baker Street and Metropolitan Line to Northwick Park shouldn't take more than an hour. I had been glad to leave the bank promptly after another boring day spent waiting for Martin to demonstrate exactly why he needed a highly qualified and expensive secretary. I was beginning to think that I was nothing more than a status symbol for him.

'So the concept is a kind of adult Andy Pandy?' I asked, as seriously as I could. 'One clown, a large inflatable bear and a dolly bird?'

'I've never thought of it like that, but yeah, great idea. I wonder if we could use that in the advertising,' replied my companion on the sofa.

He was a middle-aged man with rather greasy long, curly hair who was wearing a tight white T-shirt, white jeans and ostrich-skin cowboy boots. He said his name was Nat. He turned and whispered loudly to Mars in his strange, vaguely transatlantic accent, 'This girl's cool. Where did you find her?'

It was all I could do to keep a straight face.

'What I don't understand,' I continued, 'is where I would fit in. I mean, are we thinking clown, bear or bird?'

Both the men roared with laughter. I couldn't work out whether they were pissed or taking the piss, but I wasn't staying to find out because it was coming up to seven o'clock.

'I've got to be going,' I said, standing up and slipping on my jacket.

'I was just about to order another bottle,' said Mars.

I was quite glad to have the excuse of a hospital visit. Comedy is a small but growing world, and it's a bad idea to offend anyone, although I was doubtful that Nat would make a success of his 'high-concept alternative game show'. Even if he did, I was quite sure that I wanted nothing to do with it. Mum, Reg and I used to be regular viewers of *The Generation Game* when I was a child. Reg and I had once planned to become contestants (we had decided that Reg would be my uncle, since Brucie probably wouldn't accept a mother's boyfriend) but it had never been my ambition to be Anthea Redfern then, and it certainly wasn't now, however much Mars tried to dress up the formula, using words like parodic and post-modern.

Mars escorted me to the door and put me in a taxi.

'I'll call you first thing tomorrow and we can talk money,' he said.

'Fine,' I said, because that was how our meetings always ended.

His next line usually was, 'Did I tell you how wonderful you're looking?' And that would be my cue to blush and close the cab door, then he would disappear through the revolving door of the club, and I wouldn't hear from him for a couple of months.

*

I was quite shocked at how much Reg had aged. I had seen him only two Sundays before, when he had cut a very robust figure carving the topside. I had a clear memory of him spearing his individual Yorkshire pudding with a long-handled, two-pronged fork, holding it aloft and waving it in the air as he made an emotional speech about dog dirt on Pinner pavements. Perhaps he had been too exercised, I thought. Too exercised and not enough exercise. Or perhaps all that red meat and gravy had clogged his arteries.

He was dozing when I arrived, and his face was very vulnerable and grey against the white hospital pillow-cases. I wondered whether I should wake him. It seemed a shame to disturb him, but I had come quite a long way. I drew up a chair beside the bed, sat down and opened my *Evening Standard*. After a very short time I became aware that I was being watched by the young male nurse who was changing the sheets on the next bed.

'Let me guess . . . I'd say you were a Virgo.'

I sat up with a start, wondering how on earth he knew I had turned to the horoscopes page.

'You'd better believe it,' I replied. 'Actually, I'm a . . .'

'No, don't tell me . . . Capricorn.'

'No.'

'You sure?'

'Yes, I am sure.' If he hadn't been so very good-looking, I would have already tired of this game. I don't believe in horoscopes, of course. (Although I have found that Patric Walker is sometimes uncannily accurate . . .)

'I know . . . You have to be a Pisces.'

I tried to remember what the typical Pisces was meant to be like, and work out whether I should be flattered or offended.

'No. I'm a . . .'

'No, don't tell me. I'm really good at guessing.'

'You're not. You've been wrong about me three times already.'

'Aries, then – they're impatient.'

'No,' I said impatiently.

'Leo?'

'Oh, for heaven's sake.' We were both laughing now.

'All right, then, tell me.'

'Aquarius,' I said, and a brief, uninvited, silly hope that his star sign was something compatible flickered through my mind. Mentally, I stamped on it.

'I knew it!' he said. 'They're the elusive ones. Always the most difficult to guess. Very hard to pin down.' He nodded in Reg's direction. 'You must be his daughter, Sophie. I've heard a lot about you.'

'Have you?' It surprised me that Reg had talked about me, and I was rather touched that he referred to me as his daughter. In fact, Reg was no relation, in blood or law, to me. He had been my mother's boyfriend for twenty years or so, but they had never married. My father ran off to Paris with a waitress when I was a child. I think my mother was very wary about marrying again, but Reg became more or less a permanent fixture. While he has never attempted to take on a father's role, he has always been very kind and generous to me, and apart from politics, which we don't discuss, we get along very well together.

I didn't feel like explaining the niceties of our family arrangements, so I just sat there smiling, glowing slightly with daughterly warmth, and hoping that I had my better profile turned towards the nurse.

'I think I spoke to you yesterday.' He seemed determined to chat.

31

'Oh . . . I thought that you were a doctor.'

'Oh dear, a bit of sexual stereotyping there.'

'Certainly not!' I protested.

'You've just never met a male nurse?'

'Well, I suppose not. Not socially, anyway,' I added ridiculously, making the male ward of Northwick Park sound like a wine bar.

'Reg said you were funny. I can see what he means.'

Funny in what sense? I hadn't actually been trying to be funny, merely polite, but I didn't have a chance to point this out, since Reg was starting to wake up. His eyes took a little while to focus, but when they did, his pleasure at seeing me lit up his face. It was such an involuntary smile that I had to force back the tears that sprang to my eyes. I don't think I had ever acknowledged before that moment how much I loved Reg or how worried I had been in the knowledge that he had just narrowly missed death.

'Sophie, how are you?'

'Fine. But how are you? Feeling any better?'

'Much better, thanks. Fit as a fiddle, really, but the doctor, and my friend Dave here –' he pointed to the nurse – 'say that I'll have to take it easy for a while.'

I tried to imagine Reg doing anything else. Apart from mowing the lawn, I had never seen him engaged in any physical activity. The guiding principle of his and my mother's life was comfort, and although my mother had somehow managed to keep her reed-like figure since the sixties, Reg's penchant for sherry and television was beginning to show around the waist.

'How's the new job?' Reg asked.

I launched into a description of the bank, making it seem far more appealing than it actually was, then I started telling him about my meeting with Mars and the ageing trendy I had been drinking with in the Groucho earlier. It was quite a performance, and I realized, when I breathlessly came to the end of an anecdote, that as well as trying to cheer Reg up, I was showing off outrageously in the hope of impressing Dave, who had finished with the sheets and was standing with his arms folded, watching me.

'You do that professionally,' he said.

'She does,' said Reg proudly.

'Well, not really,' I said quickly. 'I just do a stand-up routine in a pub on Saturday nights sometimes.'

'I wouldn't mind seeing that,' said Dave. 'Is it a pub round here?'

I tried to imagine any of the huge, forbidding suburban pubs I knew in Harrow or Pinner putting on comedy nights.

'No, Islington.'

'Well, you'll have to tell me where. Excuse me, I've got to get the drugs started. The boys will be needing their fix.'

'Good-looking lad,' Reg remarked, watching my eyes follow Dave walking down the ward.

'Certainly is,' I said, then added quickly, 'if you like that sort of thing.'

That sort of thing had dark-brown hair, dark-blue eyes and perfect teeth. He had a sexy, but arrogant smile, not unlike Tom Cruise, which seemed to say two things: both 'I would like to fuck you' and 'You would like to fuck me.' I usually prefer men who look less sure of themselves.

'He's recently split up from his girlfriend,' said Reg.

'Oh, no. You're not trying to matchmake, are you?' I said with mock horror. 'He's years younger than me, for heaven's sake.'

33

'Matchmake? I'd never dare,' said Reg. 'He's twenty-four, as a matter of fact.' He had a twinkle in his eye that wasn't, I thought, entirely to do with the fact that my mother had just walked into the ward.

Chapter Four

The applause was louder than usual and somebody at the back was doing one of those finger-in-the-mouth, taxi-hailing whistles I have never been able to do. I felt rather pleased with myself. I knew that the act had improved in the months since Edinburgh, but this was the best reception I could remember at the pub. There was quite a crowd in. I allowed myself to think that it might be because the publican had finally given in to my requests for a bit of advertising. (There was a handmade poster with my photo on it pasted to a folding board on the pavement outside the pub.) I discovered when I went to buy a round later that the numbers were due to a six-pints-for-the-price-of-five offer on a new brand of Australian lager.

I bowed again, gathered up my bits and pieces and bounced off the stage, nearly bumping into a man wearing a rubber Mrs Thatcher mask who was next on. I took off my leather biker's jacket and stuffed my props – a pair of horn-rimmed spectacles, a Hermès headscarf – into a Sainsbury's shopping bag. Then I splashed some cold water on to my face from the sink in the tiny curtained-off space that the publican referred to as the green room (I presume because there was quite a lot of mould on the wall below the tap).

I crept down the side of the stage and along the back of the audience to the door into the main pub. I was looking for a spare seat when my gaze fell on a familiar face waving at me from a table near the door. Unaware that she had attracted my attention already, Jools stood up and shouted, 'Over here, Sophie! Mine's a pint of lager shandy.'

I noticed that the woman who was sharing her table finished her drink hastily and left.

The owner of the pub happened to be serving at the bar. He congratulated me on my reception and treated me to a drink.

'Several people have been asking for you tonight,' he said.

'Who?' I asked.

'A couple of blokes – I think they are still in watching . . .' He nodded towards the back room of the pub. 'One of them looked familiar. I think I've seen him here before . . . Oh, and a woman.' He looked around and nodded in Jools's direction. 'Sitting over there.'

'Thanks,' I said, wondering who the men could be.

Perhaps it was Dave, the nurse on Reg's ward. He must be very keen to see me again, I thought excitedly, because when I had tried to find him at the end of visiting time, to tell him the address of the pub, he had gone off on a coffee break. I had felt at the time it would look a bit pushy to wait.

Martin was another possibility, but I rather hoped that it wasn't him, since we had seen a bit too much of each other at work in the past week.

I had once met a past lover in this pub. For a second, I allowed myself to imagine that it might be him. No, I reasoned, if Greg did want to meet up again after more than a year, he would hardly come all the way from Dublin on the off chance of me still playing this pub.

I picked up the drinks and made my way over to Jools's

table, where she was vigorously defending the vacant seat from the attentions of a shirtless man whose beer belly was hanging over the top of his jeans.

'That's the one thing I hate about the summer,' she said heatedly as I sat down.

'What?' I inquired.

'All that disgusting flesh.'

She was wearing a multicoloured striped stretch tube that began about a foot above her knees and stopped just above almost non-existent breasts, leaving her arms and shoulders completely bare. I looked her up and down pointedly.

'Well, at least mine is not plodgy, white and covered with springy black hairs,' she said.

'True,' I conceded. 'How have you managed to get tanned so quickly?'

'It's painted on. With my colouring I haven't got a cat's chance in hell of getting a tan. But this stuff is great. Not so good if you're intending to have sweaty sex on white sheets, but that's not looking too likely tonight.'

'Don't count on it,' I said. 'Apparently two men were asking about me.' I suppressed an image of Greg that floated involuntarily through my mind.

'Oh, Gawd, a fan club! Well, that *is* a surprise.'

'Why?' I asked, slightly defensively. Like most comedians I know, I have a bit of a sense of humour vacuum when it comes to criticism of my work.

'Well, men might find some of your stuff a bit threatening, know what I mean? I mean, that Joy character. We girls know it's true, but it's not exactly flattering, is it?'

'What, you mean the stuff about New Men and oral sex . . . Where *are* you supposed to put your hands?'

'Exactly,' said Jools.

'Oh, I'm glad I got that bit right. I mean, it's been so

37

long since I had sex, I'm not sure I remember what you do.'

'It's like riding a bicycle,' said Jools.

'I think my bits must be in the wrong place, then, because I've never come cycling. Do you think that's why they called those old-fashioned bikes "sit up and beg"?'

'You're even more disgusting than me,' said Jools. 'Anyway, I loved the show, by the way. Same again?'

'Yeah, thanks.'

She got up, smoothing her dress over her enviably narrow hips.

'Cor, I'd like to suck your pussy,' one of the men at the next table called out.

'Why don't you go suck your mother's? You'd be far happier,' responded Jools without missing a beat, and sashayed over to the bar.

When I looked a few minutes later, the next table was empty.

'So, who do you think these guys are?' said Jools, taking a sip from her glass.

'Who?'

'The ones who were asking for you.'

I was half-way down my second pint of lager and had completely forgotten about them, but I was saved from wondering further as a pair of large, slightly damp hands covered my eyes and a familiar voice said, 'Guess who?'

'Well, it smells like someone who's gone a bit over-board with Obsession for Men,' I said. 'For heaven's sake, Mars, get off.'

I turned round to receive the regulation Mwaas, and was not entirely delighted to see that accompanying him was his friend from the Groucho Club, Nat.

I introduced them to Jools.

'So you're an actress too?' Nat immediately zoomed in on her, drawing up a chair from the next table.

'No.'

'But Zoe said she worked with you.'

'Sophie. And I said work out,' I interrupted.

'Yeah, babe, check,' said Nat, pulling my seat closer to Jools's, sitting down on it, leaving me standing.

'I could never be an actress,' Jools said, 'because, you see, I wet myself in the Junior nativity play at primary school and I've had stage fright ever since . . .'

Nat laughed.

'Hey, this babe's cool,' he said to no one in particular.

'Sophie. A word.' Mars drew me aside with an exaggerated air of confidentiality.

'Nat and I have been talking.'

'Speak up. I can't hear a word you're saying.'

'Nat just adores you, loves what you do, but I'll be honest . . . he's having some difficulty getting all the little pieces of finance in place.'

'Let alone the big ones,' I said.

'He really wants to come up with a vehicle for you.'

'Oh, come off it, Mars. I'm a complete unknown, who would want to give me a vehicle? I can't even drive . . .'

'Modesty becomes you, Miss Fitt. Let's all lunch soon. Kick around a few ideas.'

'Hey, guys,' said Nat, 'let's have some decent champagne!'

Knowing that the pub hardly ran to a decent house white, I suggested a nearby wine bar, but I should really have gone home right then.

The next day I could just about remember events during the first bottle, but the rest of the evening was very hazy, and a nagging worry that there had been singing at some stage only served to exacerbate my hangover.

Chapter Five

There was a memo on my desk from the computer controller, Marie, telling me that my password for the computer had changed. But the new password didn't seem to work. I called Marie but her extension was engaged, so I called Pat and asked if she would mind helping me when she had a moment.

A few minutes later she hurried over, rather flustered, saying that they were expecting a lot of activity in Eurobonds that morning, and generally making me feel guilty about asking for help, especially since the problem turned out to be that the figures I thought were zeros were in fact letter 'o's.

'Oh dear, I'm obviously not quite awake yet,' I said, embarrassed.

'Some of us have been here since six-thirty,' she replied. 'Monday's always such a hectic day. Ah, here's your boss.' She put a great deal of emphasis on the last word, then hurried back to her desk.

'Problems?' said Martin cheerily. I wondered how he always managed to look so happy arriving at work.

'Not really.' I sighed. 'I'm afraid that Pat doesn't think I'm competent or diligent enough, and I think she suspects that we're having an affair.'

'Hold on, Miss Fitt, you've only worked here a week. She'd have to think I'm a pretty fast mover.'

'Yeah, but I think she saw us outside the wine bar on my first day,' I said.

'Well, let her think what she wants. I'm technically her boss, you know. I don't have to explain myself,' he said, trying, I felt, to convince himself as much as me.

'It's not just her, though,' I continued. 'I'm sure she's told everyone else. It would be much easier for me if you just told everyone that I'm a friend of yours who's helping you out, you know. I'm sure I'm being ostracized by the dealers because they think I'm spying for you.'

'Well, you were the one who said it would undermine my authority, if people knew.'

'I know, I know.' I sighed wearily. 'I just didn't realize how long eight hours could be when no one's speaking to you.'

'Well, you'll be glad to know that I've done some work over the weekend, so there's going to be a lot for you to do,' said Martin. 'Would you mind stepping into my office, Miss Fitt?'

'Certainly, sir,' I said, smiling. I was fed up with pretending to be busy. I rang the switchboard and asked for my calls to be put through to Martin's extension until further notice.

It was an odd and not particularly pleasant experience taking dictation from Martin. His grammar is terrible and he has no sense of punctuation.

'There's no verb in that sentence,' I remarked.

'Are you always like this?' he replied quite sharply.

'I'm just trying to save you embarrassment.'

'All right, all right. But I am the boss here, you know.'

I put down my pencil and pad.

'I knew this wouldn't work,' I said. 'If you're the sort of person who has a power trip about their secretary, one, I'm not going to work for you, and, two, you should

41

bloody well know better. For heaven's sake, even when we were working on the same level as executives, half the secretaries knew more than we did, even though they were paid a pittance. Just because you're called a junior vice-president now doesn't make you any better than me. You're as new to this job as I am . . .'

'Have you finished the rant?' he asked good-humouredly.

'No.'

'Look, Soph, I know that's all true. I'm sorry I was a bit over the top, but I'm finding this just as difficult as you. Let's remember that we're doing each other a favour, and try to keep a sense of humour about the situation. I know it's weird, but we must be big enough to get over the first hurdle . . .'

'Finished the patronizing, clichéd managerial pep talk?' I inquired.

'Ouch!'

'OK.' I took up my pencil and pad again. 'Maybe it would be better, in future, if you did audio, then I could just correct your mistakes as I typed,' I added.

His phone rang. He picked it up.

'Martin Young.' He took the receiver away from his ear and stared at it.

'That's odd. The person just hung up.'

'Oh, that's happened to me three times this morning. I think it's someone who wants Denise.'

'Denise?'

'My predecessor.'

'Oh. Why don't you tell them she's not here?'

'I never get the chance. They always hang up straight away. I can hardly pick up the phone and shout "She's dead" at them before they ring off, can I?'

'I suppose not,' he said.

The phone rang again. He picked it up and listened, but didn't speak for a minute.

'She's just here. I'll hand you over,' he said, stretching across his mock-antique desk to hand me the receiver.

'Hallo?' I said.

There was silence. Then the caller hung up.

'They hung up again,' I said.

'But that wasn't for Denise,' said Martin.

'How do you know?' I asked.

'Because she asked for you. She said, "Is Sophie there?"'

I had typed about half the letters by lunchtime. They were mostly messages of greeting to all the heads of FX operations in the bank's branches round the world. They all contained the same paragraph of potted CV at the centre, but were topped and tailed by a couple of personalized sentences. Martin had obviously struggled to find something different to say to each person, and I wondered why he bothered, since someone in Seoul was presumably unlikely to discuss the wording of Martin's first inconsequential missive with someone in New York, but as the letters were keeping me legitimately occupied, I refrained from arguing the logic of this out with Martin.

I was just about to save all the files I had created that morning when my phone rang.

'Hallo. Martin Young's office.'

Nothing, but I could tell the caller had not yet hung up. I wondered whether it was Jools using one of the phones at the health club. They might be the sort where you have to press the button on answer. Whenever I used one I forgot to do that. In case she could hear me, I said, 'All right, I'll be down in about five minutes. OK?'

I couldn't find Jools anywhere in Eden and, since the

pool looked pretty crowded, I decided to take a rain check on fitness that day. To be honest, I've never been all that excited by gyms. It's not the exercise. I don't mind a game of tennis in the summer, or the occasional run in the park, but I cannot stand the proselytizing, almost religious, fervour of real gymnasium addicts. I can think of better ways of spending a lunch hour than wiping the sweat off Nautilus machines after the puffing, groaning moron with the matching Spandex vest and cycling shorts who is always in front of me on the circuit has finished his fifty leg-rises. Also, I had received a pre-publication copy of my friend Dan's second novel in the post that morning and, having read the first couple of pages on the tube, I was eager to continue.

The old graveyard was like a little green clearing in the dusty grey concrete forest of the City. All the benches were taken, but I found a quiet corner and spent an enjoyable half-hour propped up against the tombstone of one William Smithers and his beloved wife, Thomasine, totally engrossed in Dan's evocation of the gay subculture of Glasgow, and taking the occasional bite from a Marks and Spencer celery and cheese sandwich.

When I arrived back at the office, Pat informed me that the computer had gone down a couple of minutes before. I shrieked and ran into my office, realizing, too late, that I had forgotten to save my work that morning. I couldn't see her face through the smoked-glass wall of her office, but I couldn't help thinking that Pat was smiling as I hit a few buttons on my keyboard in a futile attempt to retrieve Martin's letters.

Vowing not to let this happen again, I started going through my desk drawers looking for back-up diskettes. The first two were crammed with bits and pieces of office equipment. Broken paperclips, blocks of multicoloured Post-it notes, several half-used bottles of Tippex, which must have predated the installation of the computer and were rock hard, their caps never properly replaced, a few elastic bands, several dry biros, a couple of fluorescent highlighters, which I kept, but no diskettes.

The bottom drawer was sticking out a centimetre or so. I had laddered several pairs of tights on it, but despite pulling the handle with all the force I could muster, I hadn't yet been able to open it. Thinking that I might bring more force by pulling at the same level as the handle, I lay on the floor and tugged.

Martin almost tripped over me as he came back from lunch.

'What on earth . . .?'

'Don't ask,' I snarled. The drawer still wouldn't budge.

'I'm looking for diskettes. I just lost all the work I did this morning.'

'Oh dear,' said Martin. 'To lose one letter is unfortunate, to lose them all . . .'

He faltered mid-sentence, seeing my distinctly unamused expression.

'What do these diskettes look like, then?'

'Oh, for heaven's sake, stop being such a pathetic man. They're small and square and usually grey plastic. You must have had some computer training!'

Martin walked into his office and pulled open one of the drawers in his desk.

'Like these?' he said, pulling out a new pack of twelve.

'Yes.' I snatched them from him.

I gave the bottom drawer a hard kick, as I sat down. It sprang out and hit me on the shin.

'I think this drawer's got it in for me,' I said. 'What

am I supposed to do with this lot?' I added, pulling stuff out of it.

Martin looked over my shoulder.

'Why don't you clear it all out? If there's anything personal we'll send it back to her next of kin.'

I shivered. I didn't like the idea of sifting through the dead woman's possessions.

The various bits and bobs of rubbish told a certain story of her life. I knew, for instance, that she had been watching her weight (two boxes of low-fat powdered soup, one beef-and-tomato flavour, the other asparagus with croutons; a packet of sugar-free chewing gum), she suffered from cystitis (a half-empty bottle of bicarbonate of soda), her star sign was Libra (a broken key fob), she was averagely vain and prone to perspiration (some matt face powder and a mirror), she had been planning a holiday in the Balearics (the brochures had been responsible for jamming up the drawer). There was also a breath-freshener spray, a couple of individual cartons of long-life orange juice, an expired one-month membership card to Eden, two unsigned Valentine cards (the sort I hate with cuddly animals and 'amusing' messages), and a small but hideous nude gonk (I hadn't seen one since I was at primary school) with a shock of purple nylon hair.

I couldn't imagine that the next of kin would appreciate the return of these effects. I wondered for a while about the gonk, but decided that it was so tasteless, it could only upset the grieving relatives more. Apart from the sachets of asparagus-flavour Slimma soup, which I find just about drinkable, and the orange juice, I threw everything into the bin. It seemed awful to judge someone on the basis of a mundane little pile of possessions, but I couldn't help feeling that I wouldn't have liked Denise much.

Towards the end of the afternoon, I was returning to my office, having just faxed Martin's letters all over the world, when I heard the phone ring.

'Can't you tell the switchboard when you're away from your office? Your bloody phone's annoying me,' said the dealer who sat nearest to me. They were the first words he had addressed to me since I started work. I glared at him.

'Hallo. Sophie Fitt,' I said, forgetting my usual sing-song chirrup.

There was silence, then, just as I was about to slam down the phone, a small female voice said, 'Are you OK?'

'Yes, thanks,' I replied, wondering who was asking.

'Oh, good,' she said, and replaced the receiver.

I picked up the hard-copies of the letters I had just sent and started to file them, wondering who it was who called. It wasn't a voice I recognized, but she hadn't introduced herself, so I assumed that I was meant to know. At the bottom of the pile was the memo that had appeared on my desk that morning and I realized that the woman on the phone must have been Marie, computer controller, checking to see that I was OK after the lunchtime blip.

Martin kept me pretty busy for the rest of the week. On one occasion I even worked through my lunch hour. But nothing I did seemed to please Pat. When I was working hard, I think she felt threatened by the potential of another office martyr usurping her position, and she would issue friendly advice when we coincided in the

loos about the dangers of repetitive strain injury. Whenever I arrived in the office a few minutes late, she
couldn't stop herself glancing at the row of clocks, which
showed my delay in triplicate.

Jools rang me on Friday, apologizing for missing a whole
week at the gym. She said that the stylist had decided
the untypical summer weather was just too hot to take
exterior shots of winter clothes, so they had all been
shipped off to a stately home in Norfolk to do the interior
shots. It was quite a pile, she said, with a walled garden
and an outdoor swimming pool, but they were miles
away from anywhere and there was nothing to do in the
evenings except bicker with the other models. We arranged to meet at lunchtime on Monday.

I like to have all my work completed and filed at the end
of each week. It's a habit I have picked up since working
as a temp because I often find myself working for week-
long stints, replacing someone who's ill. I can't bear to
think of them struggling in on Monday morning, feeling
groggy, to find their desk in a mess. My small nod
towards worker solidarity, however, often means that I
finish late on Fridays. Everything in the City closes
promptly on a Friday and there's a kind of post-neutron-
bomb feeling about the deserted streets.

   I walked towards Moorgate station. The only signs of
life were the rumble of drinking noise and cigarette
smoke emanating, like a burp, from the doors of a pub,
and a lone window dresser, silently working behind the
glass frontage of a women's clothes shop. He had already
changed some of the mannequins out of summer dresses
and shorts into warmer autumn wear. He was struggling
with a hacking jacket and a particularly recalcitrant

mannequin whose stiff joints seemed unwilling to countenance rough tweed on such a hot evening. I laughed, thinking of Jools and her mocking description of herself last weekend as a clotheshorse.

It didn't occur to me until later that it was funny, if winter clothes were already going into the shops, that Jools and her friends were still being photographed for autumn catalogues.

I didn't really dwell on it then, because I was on a Friday evening high myself. I was going to dinner in Pinner. Reg had been discharged from hospital earlier in the week and my mother was cooking a cholesterol-free supper to celebrate his recovery.

Chapter Six

I bought a bottle of Aqua Libra, as I wasn't sure whether Reg was supposed to be drinking alcohol, as well as some champagne.

'Bloody awful stuff, gives me wind,' said the owner of the off-licence.

'Champagne?' I asked.

'Nah, that herbal stuff. All it is is a bit of water with some new-fangled flavouring, and they're charging the price of a perfectly adequate Frascati. I'm surprised people are so daft.'

I handed over my money, rather regretting that I hadn't gone to Sainsbury's. The booze was cheaper there and the anonymous check-out girls didn't make you feel like a fool for succumbing to advertising. But I had known the off-licence owner since my childhood and felt a sense of misplaced loyalty.

'It's for Reg. He may not be drinking, you know, after hospital . . .'

'I took him in a couple of individual gin and tonics when I visited,' said the owner, winking. 'They didn't seem to do him any harm.'

'Well, I quite like it anyway,' I said, feeling I had in some way to defend my purchase, and held out my hand to take the plastic carrier bag.

'Hang on a mo. Give him this, with my regards,' said the proprietor.

It was a bottle of good claret. 'I was reading an article

the other day which said the French get fewer heart attacks due to the old *vin rouge* . . .'

'Yeah, liver disease gets them before they're old enough for heart attacks,' I said and smiled sweetly.

The door bell, which can play ninety-nine tunes and was installed by Reg one Christmas as a surprise present for Mum, was programmed to sound the first ten notes of 'Summertime'. It annoyed me more than usual because that is one of my favourite songs. I can just about put up with 'Jingle Bells' reduced to a few nerve-grating, computer-generated sounds at Christmas, but this was almost offensive. My mother opened the door.

'Honestly, Mum, you should accidentally-on-purpose break that bloody bell. It's embarrassing,' I said, walking past her.

'Don't you like it?' she replied equably. 'You look smart.'

I did a little twirl in my terracotta-linen shorts suit.

'I think I'd wear it with a white blouse,' she said, appraising me.

I looked in the hall mirror and realized that, as usual, she was right. The primrose-yellow silk blouse didn't really do anything for me against my pale skin. My mother has impeccable taste when it comes to clothes.

She was dressed in a Liberty lawn dress with a lace collar and looked very summery. I have never worked out how my mother manages to sit in skirts without crumpling them. She always looks perfectly newly laundered and ironed, so much so that when I reached to kiss her, the Coco perfume she wears almost came as a surprise, as I was expecting the fresh smell of starch.

'How's the invalid?' I asked.

'Seems a lot better,' said Mum and smiled at me. It

was a slightly odd smile that contained an element of secrecy. It said there was something that she wasn't telling me.

'What?' I asked.

'What what?' she said disingenuously.

'Why are you smiling like that?' I said.

'Everything in good time,' she said. 'You're always so impatient.'

In order to demonstrate that she was wrong, I said nothing for a few minutes, and then, unable to bear the suspense, whined, 'Oh, come on, Mum, tell me . . .'

'No,' she said firmly. 'We'll tell you together. Reg is having a nap. It's a cold supper, so we'll wait until he wakes.'

'You're what?' I was so surprised that the piece of sea bass I had just put in my mouth lurched towards my windpipe and I started coughing.

Reg jumped up and hit me several times on the back. Mum rushed into the kitchen to get a glass of water.

'I went through it with the tweezers . . .' she said.

'What?' I asked, calming down.

'Getting the bones out. I know how you hate fish with bones in.'

'It's not a bone. It just went down the wrong way,' I said, sipping the water. 'I'm a bit shocked, that's all. The fish is wonderful.'

She had poached the whole fish lightly then poured a marinade of dry sherry, soy sauce and finely chopped fresh ginger and spring onion over it as it cooled. A salad of blanched mangetout and shitake mushrooms accompanied the fish, along with some slightly oversteamed rice.

'What made you decide? I mean, you've had a pretty long courtship,' I said.

'Not for want of me asking,' said Reg gently.

My mother smiled at me, but her eyes carried the message, don't press it, I'll tell you later.

'Well, congratulations!' I said and held up my glass. 'I'm sure you'll be very happy together. You always have been, as long as I've known you.' Everything I was saying was sounding so clichéd, I faltered with embarrassment, but how are you supposed to react when your mother announces that she is about to marry the man she has been going out with for over twenty years?

'Do you want me to give you away?' I joked.

'Well, actually, we would like you to be bridesmaid,' my mother said.

I laughed out loud, then realized that she was being perfectly serious.

'You're not having a church wedding?' I said in astonishment.

'Well, not exactly. But there will be a blessing. It's a bit difficult to have the whole wedding thing if you're divorced. We didn't want to embarrass the vicar, so we thought just a blessing, after the registry office. It means I can have the "Wedding March". I always wanted that. You know, first time round, it was Chelsea Registry Office with Marcus in jeans and me six months gone with you. I'd like to do it properly this time.'

As my mother rattled on about arrangements (have you ever noticed how boring people get about weddings? You can think you're having a perfectly intelligent conversation and they suddenly interrupt with something like 'The florist's being wonderfully supportive' or 'I talked to the cake-icer today. She says she thinks a lattice design will go better with my dress'), I tried to think up an excuse to get out of being her bridesmaid. I was pleased that they were getting married – it seemed a rather romantic thing to do at their age – but I couldn't stand the idea of dressing up in a frilly dress.

I had been a bridesmaid twice before. Once when I was eight years old, which was fine. I wore an ice-blue dress with a Peter Pan collar and, with my long blonde hair, I look a little like Alice in Wonderland in the photos. And once when I was thirteen, which was a disaster. It was Reg's sister who had been getting married. I was going through a difficult patch as I entered puberty. I think they thought it would be nice to include me in some way, and as she was having so many bridesmaids, it would have been very pointed not to ask me, but the wedding had coincided with the arrival of my first period and an outbreak of acne, and I had spent the entire day rushing to the loo, either to apply concealing stick to my spots or to check that I wasn't leaking on my lilac dress. Fortunately, one of my visits to the ladies coincided with the pictures being taken, so there is no record of my attendance.

'I really think I'm a bit old to be a bridesmaid,' I said tentatively when there was a pause in the plans for the reception.

'Nonsense. You don't look twenty-eight anyway,' said Reg, adding hurriedly, 'Not that twenty-eight's old, of course.'

'I just think that maybe people will think it's a bit silly.'

'Oh,' said my mother, obviously disappointed. 'I had seen such a nice dress for you too.'

'I'm really pleased for you and all that,' I persisted, 'but it's just . . .'

'It's OK. I thought you might not,' said Mum. 'Perhaps you could have the dress anyway . . .'

'Oh, really, no. I'll get something myself,' I said hastily.

'It's Vivienne Westwood, I think. Kind of old-gold silk – looks a bit Regency, or something. It would suit you. Oh, well. It was only an idea. You please yourself. You usually do.'

Now that she had described it, the dress did sound rather wonderful. But I could hardly go back on my protestations. Silence hung around us for a moment or two, then I collected myself and said brightly, 'What about your dress?'

'Not in front of the groom,' said Mum, adding, 'What do you think of this fool?' to change the subject.

I said it was lovely. The gooseberries were from the garden and Mum had added a splash of elderflower cordial. I wondered whether it was the sort of thing that Reg should be eating, as it tasted quite creamy.

'Low-fat fromage frais,' said Mum, as if reading my mind. 'Come on, help me with the washing-up, and I'll tell you about my outfit.'

I was drying the fish kettle, while Mum wiped down the surfaces, and Reg was safely ensconced out of earshot watching Wimbledon highlights in the front room.

'What made you decide, then?' I asked.

'Well, I suppose it was the stress,' she said.

'Stress?' I repeated, checking that I had heard her correctly. Apart from carrying a few trays of bedding plants back from Homebase, I couldn't imagine Reg suffering any stress.

'The doctor said he was under a lot of stress. Apparently he had talked to Reg and asked if there was anything worrying him in his life, and Reg said that he was always anxious about his relationship with me. He seemed to think that just because I didn't want to marry him, I was about to walk off at any moment . . .'

55

'Oh, how sweet!'

'Well, the doctor had a quiet word with me and I thought, well, if it's giving the man a heart attack, I ought to do the decent thing and make an honest man of him . . .'

Mum had obviously practised this witticism, because she said it with a kind of flourish and paused afterwards waiting for my laughter. I obliged.

'Then the difficult thing was getting him to ask me again . . .'

'Couldn't you have asked him?' I realized it was a silly question almost before the words were out of my mouth. My mother may have been a sixties raver, but feminism seemed to have passed her by (although, I must say, she always gets what she wants).

'There's this lovely place where they sometimes have dinner dances. The last time Reg asked me was there, so I made a reservation for dinner. Not dancing, of course, he can't do that until after his first check-up, and I rang up to see whether they had any low-cholesterol dishes . . . Anyway, it was lovely. We were sitting outside under this kind of canopy of trailing roses, and I said to Reg, "This would be a lovely place to have a wedding reception, wouldn't it?"'

'Subtle,' I interrupted.

'Well, it was a bit too subtle as it turned out, because he ignored that comment. I think he didn't want to be disappointed again, you see, so I pressed on. "Do you remember what you asked me last time we were here?" I said. "I hadn't forgotten my wallet, had I?" said Reg, but I could see he was beginning to catch on. There was a bit of a twinkle in his eye. So we went on like this for a while, and finally I said that it was so nice having him out of hospital and I was so happy that I'd probably agree to anything he suggested. So he went down on one knee, and the chef sent out a selection of sorbets to celebrate . . .'

Mum's eyes were shining. She was obviously very happy. Then a frown crossed her face.

'Oh, thank goodness you refused to be a bridesmaid,' she exclaimed.

'Why?'

'Well, I just remembered. You've done it twice already, haven't you? And you know what they say? Three times a bridesmaid, never a bride . . .'

'Oh, for heaven's sake!' I said. 'What a load of rubbish. That's just about enough to make me change my mind.' I looked at Mum and saw a flicker of triumph on her face.

'You said that deliberately, didn't you? Just to get a rise out of me? All right then, I tell you what. I'll wear a pretty dress and I'll be your witness at the registry office, but I'm not prancing down the aisle behind you. OK?'

'OK,' Mum agreed. 'And I'll just have to make sure you catch my bouquet.'

Chapter Seven

I found myself thinking a lot about my father over the weekend. I suppose all the talk about weddings had made me dwell on rites of passage and family stuff. I don't know quite why, but somehow I felt that my father should know that my mother was getting married again. When I had raised the subject as we were making a pot of tea after dinner, Mum hadn't agreed. She had long been over the shock of his leaving, but she had never forgiven him for losing contact with me. She had been quite perplexed at my recent attempt to establish contact, and had made it clear that she would not be involved in any reunion. It wasn't that she hated him. If she ever recalled their sixties romance it was with affection and a kind of amused disbelief that she could have been so wild, but it was as if, for her, he had ceased to exist as a person when he stopped sending me his distinctive hand-painted postcards when I was about ten. Mum is a very tolerant woman, but when she makes up her mind about something, there's no changing it.

For a long time I had blanked him out of my life too, but in my first temp job after leaving the bank I happened to work for someone who had known my father in the sixties. She was a wonderful raconteuse and some of her descriptions had brought Marcus Fitt to life for me again. Sadly she died soon after I met her. Well, I say died, but whatever the jury finally decided, I will always believe she was killed. Anyway, even though I hadn't known her very well, her death had upset me enormously and it had also made me peculiarly keen to meet my father. I suppose I had become a bit preoccupied with the fragility of life, and I wanted to meet him before he died without me ever knowing him.

I decided to write him another letter. It was a hot day and I spent too long in the sun engrossed in trying to compose something that might elicit a response. As a result, my routine at the pub was a bit lacklustre that evening and when I came to go to bed on Saturday evening I found I had to lie on my front, as my back was painfully pink and burnt.

I woke up late on Sunday, read through the letter to my father again and decided to go and post it before I changed my mind. I showered and dressed in a very large white T-shirt and linen drawstring trousers. The effect, I noticed in my cheval mirror, was not exactly flattering – being short, I can really only afford to have one baggy half, top or bottom – I looked like a hospital orderly about to compete in a sack race, but the burnt backs of my legs felt comfortable.

On my way downstairs, I couldn't help overhearing another row going on in the first-floor flat.

'It's not the adultery itself, Simon,' wailed the woman, 'it's the deception.'

'Deceit,' shouted the man. 'The word is deceit, not deception.'

It seemed a strange time to be correcting her vocabulary. What a bastard, I thought.

'I'm sorry,' said the woman miserably. 'I'll try again.'

Don't be sorry, kick him out, I thought, opening the front door and stepping out into another boiling-hot summer's day.

*

I posted my letter, bought the Sunday papers and decided to sit on Primrose Hill to read them rather than going back to my own roof terrace, where I was bound to be disturbed by the couple downstairs fighting. I would have to have a word with Costas if they kept on like this, I thought, suddenly irrationally annoyed with him that he hadn't found a nice quiet person to be a tenant, but then reasoning that I had been rather spoilt, living for several years in a flat with no neighbours.

I turned to the business sections. These days I didn't really need to keep up to date with financial stories, but five years of working in an American bank and being grilled every Monday morning at our team meeting had necessitated a habit that was hard to kick. I read quite an interesting article speculating that the Japanese stock market was about to take a dive, and felt perversely excited at the prospect. Since I had been working for Martin, the markets had been pretty steady. I had never been in a dealing room when things got really busy, but I had seen what happened in films and I would be disappointed if there was no real action during my contract.

Chapter Eight

His dark head moved slowly up my thigh, licking each millimetre in softly caressing circles. His hands gripped my buttocks and squeezed gently as his lips moved nearer my . . .

'Sophie, wake up!'

I sat up with a start, causing waves to break over the sides of the hot tub.

'I wasn't asleep,' I said.

'Oh, no?' Jools looked down at me with a knowing smile. 'Having a nice time, were you? I've always suspected men of wanking in the Jacuzzi, but a nice girl like you . . .'

'Whatever gave you the impression I was nice? Anyway, I was just having an innocent little fantasy.'

'I've often wondered whether, if men do, in there, you know what I mean, you could get pregnant if you were in there at the same time. That's why I never go near it,' said Jools.

'Ugh. Artificial insemination by a whirlpool. Sounds like something from Greek mythology,' I said.

'Gives you broken veins as well,' said Jools.

I was dressed and ready to go to lunch in less than five minutes. My hair is cut in a short bob that won't curl under however much anyone tries to blow-dry it, so I always leave it wet.

Jools took a long time with various cleansers, moisturizers and cosmetics. Her face was quite startlingly different when made up. Her complexion, which was naturally slightly greasy and prone to spots, became eggshell smooth, her large mouth, which always seemed to be talking or laughing, became a sophisticated pout as she slicked on scarlet lipstick and blotted it with a tissue. She used very little mascara, telling me that a lot of colour round the eye was ageing.

'You should take more care of your skin, before it gets too late,' she said, handing me a pot of Visible Difference.

'You sound like my mother,' I said. 'I'm twenty-eight, I haven't got a line on my face, and I'm constantly being given doom-laden prophecies about how one day I'll wake up and be sorry . . . You're pawns in the hands of advertisers.'

'You have got a few lines, as a matter of fact.'

'What?' I shoved my face right up against the mirror, giving the lie to my nonchalance. 'Where?'

'Joke,' said Jools. She pulled a lime-green muslin tunic over her white body and cycling shorts, slipped her feet into lime-green sling-back stilettos, executed a few poses in front of the mirror, and finally judged herself ready to leave.

'Shall we go back to that salt-beef place?' she asked. 'I'm tired of all this healthy food. After a while everything tastes the same. D'you know what I mean?'

'Yeah. New-mown hay,' I agreed.

'Job all right?' said Jools, biting into an apricot Danish.

'S'pose so,' I replied half-heartedly. 'I'm making inroads into the dealers. One of them even laughed at one of my jokes this morning, but it's a terrible atmosphere there. And there's not a lot to do.'

I had spent most of the morning on a call to Dan, telling him how much I had liked his second novel.

'And they keep checking up on me.'

'What d'you mean?'

'Well, there's this woman who's in charge of the computer who keeps ringing and asking if I'm OK. She sounds friendly enough, but I feel like she's checking to see if I'm at my desk, you know.'

After Dan and I had said our goodbyes, the phone had rung just once, as if to let me know that my hour-long personal call had been noted.

'What about your boss? What's he like?' asked Jools.

'Martin? He's fine, thanks. Oh, didn't I tell you? He's a friend of mine, you see. I'm helping him out, because he's new, and he's helping me out, because of my subsidence.'

'Your what?'

'My flat. It's sinking into the London clay. It's costing a fortune to prop up.'

'So your mate's employing you, but he doesn't want the other staff to know, in case they think he's bonking his secretary . . .'

'Except we don't bonk. He really is just a friend. So it's all a bit silly really.' It was quite a relief to finally tell someone.

'What a palaver,' said Jools.

I pulled my chair round to face the sun.

'How's the catalogue coming along?' I asked.

'Nearly finished now,' she said.

'Won't they have to get a move on?' I inquired.

'What do you mean?'

'Well, all the shops are full of autumn clothes already.'

'Yeah,' said Jools, then added, 'You didn't think it was for this year, did you? They work so far ahead now.'

'So, come on, give me a sneak preview,' I said.

'What d'you mean?'

'Well, what is the discerning woman going to be wearing next winter?'

'A lot of black again. To tell you the truth, I don't really notice. They're all out of my price range anyway. That's a nice dress, by the way.'

It was a royal-blue Yves St Laurent sun dress with a square neckline and gold buttons down the front. My mother had pressed it on me as I was leaving on Friday evening, saying she wished I would have it, because she found the colour a little bright. She had passed several expensive items of her clothing on to me in the last couple of years, none of which looked as if they had been worn. I was beginning to suspect that it was her way of buying me nice clothes, knowing that I was broke but that I would be far too proud to accept gifts.

'Thanks,' I said. 'My mother used to be a model, sort of.'

My mother won a competition in a women's magazine when she was a child, and her perfect face had advertised soap throughout her youth. She had been so beautiful that when my father, who is an artist, happened upon her in a Soho coffee bar in the early sixties, he had asked to paint her.

I thought I detected a frown flicker across Jools's face.

'A bit of advice,' she said. 'You ought to be wearing tights. Your legs look like crabsticks.'

I burst out laughing at the aptness of her description.

As I walked into my office, my phone rang.

'Nice lunch?' asked the woman.

'Yes, thank you. Not that it's any of your business,' I said.

I slammed down the phone.

What a bloody nerve, I thought. It was only ten minutes past two. How did she know that I hadn't left for lunch late? I hadn't. But how was she to know that? Was Pat noting down my comings and goings, I wondered? Or was it the grumpy receptionist, Dawn, who was grassing on me? I was getting sick of being checked up on. This morning, when I'd arrived practically on time, my phone had rung as soon as I had sat down and Marie's voice had said, 'Oh, *there* you are. I was just wondering . . .'

And as if that wasn't bad enough, she had forgotten whatever feeble pretext she had for calling and hung up.

When Martin arrived back from lunch I stormed into his office after him.

'I'm being harassed,' I told him angrily, explaining the situation.

He listened patiently, and agreed that it was unfair.

'I'll have a word,' he said, at the end of my rant.

And whatever he said seemed to work, because I wasn't hassled for at least two weeks after that.

Chapter Nine

It must have been shortly before Mum's wedding that the calls started again, because I remember talking about them with Dave. We were exchanging views on the new Telecom campaign, which was urging the nation to pick up the phone. The saucy advertising had caused some debate in the press, and although most people seemed to disapprove of the campaign, everyone was talking about it.

'I know someone who's taking that advice quite literally,' I said. 'They pick up the phone several times a day. Trouble is, they don't actually speak. Well, I say I know someone. I don't know them exactly.'

Dave looked at me curiously, so I began to explain.

'In the beginning,' I said, picking a piece of mint out of the bottom of my glass of Pimm's and chewing it, 'I thought it was the computer controller checking up on me. But then I met the computer controller, Marie, and realized it couldn't be her. Marie is Scottish and she has an unmistakable accent. To be honest, I can sometimes barely understand her. She says it's a common problem, so that's why she sends round memos.'

'What does your caller sound like, then?' asked Dave.

'Well, quite often she doesn't speak at all, but I kind of know she's there. When she does, her voice is absolutely nondescript. A very ordinary voice. Very occasionally she gets a bit adventurous and asks me what I'm doing, but mostly it's hallo, how are you? That kind of thing.'

When I had realized that the calls were not from Marie I had heaved a huge sigh of relief for a day or two.

Then, as they became more and more frequent, I became curious.

At first I thought it might be some weird joke of Jools's, but she strenuously denied it, and she had a huge curiosity about all the details, which I felt she wouldn't have had if she had in fact been the perpetrator.

She guessed that it might be one of the lads from the dealing room who fancied me. She said she had once experienced something similar herself when she had turned down the offer of a drink from a photographer. She was mystified when I told her the caller was a woman.

I had racked my brains to think of a woman, whose voice was not familiar to me, who might have a reason to pester me with anonymous calls. Had I, for instance, made too many bitchy remarks about one of my former colleagues? I couldn't think of anyone recently who would know where I now worked. Was it, perhaps, the wife of someone with whom I had once had an affair? No. It couldn't be. For a start, I had only ever had one affair. His wife was American, and in any case, why would someone with a thirst for revenge be so friendly?

'You don't seem very worried,' said Dave.

'Funnily enough,' I said, 'I'm not.' I probably seemed more blasé to Dave than I actually felt, but, at that stage, I really wasn't very disturbed by the phone calls.

'It sort of fascinates me,' I told him. 'It's more like a game than a threat. Sooner or later I'm bound to realize who's doing it. It's a bit like waiting for the card in Cluedo that will complete the picture.'

'You wouldn't be so casual if it was a man's voice.'

'You're probably right,' I said and smiled at him.

If anything, Dave was more handsome in a suit than in his uniform.

Although I hadn't seen him since we first met in Northwick Park Hospital, I hadn't managed to keep him entirely out of my mind, and he kept appearing in my fantasies. I wasn't, at that point, besotted enough to call him myself, but I was quite pleased to see his name on the guest list.

The service had been much more moving than I expected. As it was a simple blessing, my mother and Reg walked to the altar hand in hand. When I first caught sight of them standing at the back of the church and waiting for the music to begin, I had to gulp to keep back the tears. My mother was standing in a pool of sunlight. Her dress, which I had only glimpsed in its tissue wrapper hanging in the cupboard of the spare bedroom, was made of silk the colour of vanilla ice-cream. The bodice was very plain with a high neckline and long, slim sleeves with a row of pearl buttons from elbow to wrist. The skirt fell from just below her small bust in a column of the finest pleats. All she needed to become a princess in a fairy-tale was one of those long conical hats with a veil spilling out of the end, but with her usual immaculate taste she had merely wound her long pale-gold hair into a French pleat, securing it with pearl-tipped pins. She carried a bunch of tiny yellow roses and trailing ivy.

I wish I could say that Reg looked like a handsome prince in his morning suit. I'm sure a lot of women would have thought him a fine figure of a man, but personally I've always hated moustaches, so spruce is about the best word I can conjure up to describe him.

*

Mum finally got her 'Wedding March', and I walked up the aisle after the ceremony behind the happy couple on Martin's arm, causing all sorts of speculation, I'm sure, among the members of the Pinner WI, as well as (I was sure I noticed) a look of disappointment on Dave's face.

The dress Mum had insisted on buying me was really gorgeous and not like anything I had ever owned before, but it was a bit difficult to wear. It was rose-gold raw silk, with a stiffened bodice. It was cut away almost to my nipples and had the effect of shoving my small breasts very high and giving me a cleavage that somehow still managed to look demure, like a character in a televised Jane Austen novel. The gathered skirt, which was gloriously rough and nubbly to the touch, came to my ankles. With wanton extravagance, my mum had bought me a pair of elegant little laced boots made of the same fabric. My hair was too short to get into a pleat, but my hairdresser had swept it back with combs and, at the start of the day, I looked as sophisticated as I had ever done in my life.

It was lucky that the weather held, because Reg had hired a fleet of vintage cars to drive the guests to the reception at the country-house hotel where Mum had proposed. By the time we arrived my combs had blown away and my hair was back to its bob, but I noticed that Mum's French pleat was still intact, apart from a few wisps that had escaped and served only to make her look prettier.

Mum, who has always had a soft spot for Martin, insisted that he stand in the family line-up, greeting the rest of the guests.

'How shall I describe you?' she asked him hopefully.

'How about an old family friend?' suggested Martin, to my enormous relief.

We seemed to spend hours chatting to each one of Mum and Reg's friends in turn. Martin is terribly good at that sort of thing and if he ends up having as many rounds of golf as he agreed to that day, he'll be booked up every weekend until the turn of the century. Inevitably, there were remarks along the lines of 'You'll have to make sure that she catches Christine's bouquet', but Martin merely smiled, shook hands robustly and said things like, 'Christine's looking radiant, isn't she?', which seemed to satisfy most people.

As I watched Martin chatting to Reg's best friend, Arnie, who owns a garage, I could see why Mum thought we'd be the perfect match. One of the reasons we get on so well together is that we're both from suburban backgrounds, and although we can be as scathing as hell about Pinner or Sidcup, we recognize some of the good things about where we come from and have given up being ashamed of it. Most of the people I knew at Cambridge came from central London and in my first couple of years I quickly learned to say that I came from north London rather than Pinner. Even recently, when Mum had told me that I was welcome to invite as many friends as I wanted to the wedding, I decided to bring only Martin. Donny and Dan, whom I love dearly, wouldn't have been able to resist camping it up, relishing the hotel decorations and the unintentionally kitsch hats of some of my mother's friends. There are days when I join in such snobbish displays, but my mum's wedding was not going to be one of them.

'We must have that round of golf sometime soon,' Martin was saying. I decided to rescue him.

'Arnie. I think Stella's looking for you,' I said and presented Martin with a glass of Pimm's.

'Thanks for being such a sport,' I said. 'Now who would you really like to talk to?'

'You. We never get a chance to have a proper chat these days,' said Martin, wiping his brow and downing his Pimm's. Like a good hostess I went to get him another, but by the time I came back he was ensconced in conversation with Arnie's nineteen-year-old daughter. It looked like three would be a crowd.

'Hallo, do you remember me?' Dave tapped me on my shoulder.

'Of course,' I said.

'Is that your boyfriend?' asked Dave, nodding towards Martin with his head.

'No. He's just a friend,' I said casually, feeling rather treacherous. Martin wasn't my boyfriend but 'just a friend' didn't begin to describe him either, especially since, for the last two months, he had been my boss too. I decided it was too complicated to explain, and I noticed Reg was beckoning me over, because we were being asked to take our places at the table.

The table settings, which my mother had designed, were shallow crystal bowls crammed with Peace roses in various stages of bloom, from fully out, palely lemon with just a smudge of pink at the edges, right through to tight dark-gold buds. The buffet table was garlanded with swathes of ivy, and the food echoed the pastel colours – poached salmon, coronation chicken, tiny waxy new potatoes – along with huge bowls of dark-green salads.

Reg must have negotiated warehouse prices from his friend at the off-licence, because champagne flowed throughout the meal. I was beginning to yearn for something to drink that didn't contain bubbles when the speeches started.

I had asked Mum whether she wanted me to make a

71

kind of best-woman speech, since I was her only close family at the wedding, but she declined, saying that she would prefer me to have a nice relaxing day. (Secretly, I think she felt that any speech I would make might shock. She and Reg had come to only one of my gigs and pronounced it 'a bit blue' afterwards.) I took her at her word and found myself feeling very mellow indeed – in fact, I was so relaxed I was beginning to nod off slightly during Arnie's best-man toast. Martin elbowed me sharply in the ribs and I sat up quickly and suppressed a burp. I don't think anyone noticed.

We all went outside on to the terrace to watch Mum and Reg cut the cake, which was a two-tiered affair with pale-lemon icing and more roses on top, and in the time that it took for the photographer to capture every angle of the cake plus every combination of friend and relative, the dining hall had been cleared and the band was playing a sixties medley.

One of Mum and Reg's great pleasures is ballroom dancing and so they were able to start things off with a beautifully executed quickstep to the tune of 'Congratulations', but the dancing soon degenerated and by the time Dave plucked up the courage to ask me, I'm afraid most people were just jogging up and down in time (or not) to vaguely recognizable cover versions of early Motown. I suspected that Reg had chosen the band. I've never trusted his judgement in music since he bought that door bell.

'I'm hot!' I shouted at Dave at the end of 'Baby Love'. 'Shall we go and get something to drink?'

I couldn't face another glass of champagne. I craved a glass of home-made still lemonade, but I had to make do with tap water. I drank three glasses in quick succession.

It had been a perfect summer's day and the air was suffused with the fragrance of the honeysuckle that climbed all over the trellises above us. I inhaled deeply and sighed.

Beyond the terrace, a well-tended lawn sloped away towards an avenue of trees, beyond which was a small lake. It was beginning to get dark.

'Shall we have a look round the gardens?' asked Dave.

I nodded. We strolled down the lawn, pausing to admire the well-established herbaceous borders.

When I was a little girl, my mother used to take me for country walks near Amersham, so I know the names of wild flowers; then when Reg became a permanent fixture he taught me about gardens. The fact that I could distinguish fuchsia from delphinium seemed a cause of wonder to Dave.

'What are those called, then?' he asked, pointing.

'I don't know the Latin name,' I replied, 'but everyone calls them red hot pokers.'

For some reason this made me blush and I was glad that the garden seemed almost dark. I looked back at the hotel. Someone had turned on little coloured lights around the terrace. The music was now only a background noise. Somewhere near us a cricket chirruped.

'Shall we be getting back?' I said.

'Oh, let's just get as far as the lake,' Dave said.

I don't know whether it was the drink or the fact that there was only the tiniest sliver of a new moon to light our path, but neither of us saw the ha-ha until we were in it. I caught the hem of my dress with my heel as I went down, jerking the rigid bodice down with it and allowing one of my breasts to slip out. I landed on my elbow and shrieked with pain. Dave was immediately by my side, taking stock of the situation with the relaxed attitude of a professional. I noticed he was far more comfortable in the role of nurse than he was as wedding guest.

On his instructions, I lay in silence as he unlaced my boots and extracted each foot, gently turning each ankle to see that there was no damage. Then he clambered up the bank to deal with my arms.

'Did you hit your head?' he asked, smoothing my hair back, feeling for bumps.

'I don't think so,' I said weakly. 'It's my arm that really hurts.'

'OK,' he said. First he took the right arm, which was not hurting, swivelled the wrist, brought the hand into the air, then put it behind my head and back down by my side. Then, with the gentlest touch, he took my left arm. Supporting the elbow on his kneeling thigh, he pulled each finger in turn, then tried to swivel the wrist.

'Ow,' I shouted.

'OK, OK,' he said. 'I think you may have broken it.'

'Oh, shit,' I said and burst into tears.

'Hey, don't cry. I'm sure it's not a bad fracture. I think it's the elbow, which means that it has to heal on its own. You won't even have to have a plaster. Maybe just a sling.' He extracted the pink hanky that matched his tie from his top pocket and dabbed at my eyes.

'I'm sorry,' I said.

'It's OK,' he said. 'I'm used to it, you know.'

I smiled and sniffed.

'Do you feel strong enough to get up? I'll phone a taxi and take you to Casualty, if you like.'

'Actually, I'm quite enjoying just lying here quietly,' I said. 'Do we have to go straight away? Everyone will make such a fuss.'

He lay down beside me, staring at the starry sky, occasionally glancing at me solicitously.

It took a few seconds for it to dawn on me that I was lying on a sloping bank, out of sight of the wedding party, dishevelled, with no shoes on and one breast exposed, with a man I hardly knew but fancied like mad. I looked at him. He looked at me. I don't know who made the first move. It felt simultaneous.

I've never enjoyed making love on grass before particularly, because there always seems a lot of grazed skin afterwards, but my beautiful raw silk dress acted as a kind of groundsheet. It was probably the best snog I have ever had. Dave was starting to peel my cream stockings from their lacy self-stay tops, when I stopped him.

'No,' I said, making a great effort to sound sincere.

'Why?' he said and smiled his sexy, arrogant smile.

'They'll see us.'

'They won't. It's dark.'

'I just can't at my mother's wedding,' I said, sitting up.

'OK,' he said, 'on one condition.' He pushed me back down on to the slope. 'That the event is postponed, not cancelled.'

'You've got a deal,' I replied.

Chapter Ten

I've never really had a friend like Jools before. Maybe it's because I went to a predominantly male college at Cambridge that all my closest confidants have been gay men. Then there's Martin, of course, and I do have female friends, like Stephanie, whom I lived next to in college for a year. I don't think I'm one of those women who calls herself a feminist as an excuse to flirt with the men at a dinner party while the other women are washing up in the kitchen, but for some reason I have never really had a girlie buddy with whom I could compare contraceptive methods, or hairdressers, or spend entire lunch hours analysing why men are such bastards.

Jools had finished work on the catalogue, but she still had the occasional photographic assignment in the City, and whenever she was around she would pop into Eden for a work-out and ring me up to see if I wanted lunch.

'Did he say he'd call?' she asked.

'Yes. That's the whole point. I wouldn't have *minded* if he hadn't said anything –' this was not technically true – 'but he made this big thing about taking my number and it's been three days. Four if you count today.'

'You can't count today, because you've still got this evening.'

'Yeah, but I'm going out this evening,' I said.

'You've got an answerphone, haven't you?'

'Yeah. But I think it may not be working properly.'

Why did I always suspect my answerphone of breaking

down the minute I was on the point of starting a relationship with a man?

'Did you actually . . .?'

'No . . . You see, I was kind of waiting for him to ask me back,' I explained.

It was about midnight when we left Accident and Emergency. There had been a notice up when we arrived saying that there would be a four-hour wait, but Dave was friends with the night receptionist and I was seen, X-rayed and put in a sling in less than an hour. My arm wasn't actually broken, but it was sprained and badly bruised. We hung around outside the hospital for a while, neither of us quite sure what to suggest. Dave had become rather silent and awkward, and didn't seem inclined to invite me home, even though that would have been the obvious move. I didn't think my dress was appropriate for the last tube home on a Saturday night. I looked like one of the drunken Sloane Rangers we used to see wandering around Cambridge at breakfast-time during the May Ball season. There was no way I could return to Mum's house in Pinner on her wedding night. They were flying to Naples the next morning, and then on to Capri. Mum felt that Reg could do with a reasonable night's sleep at home to recover from the day's excitement.

The drink, dancing, injury and – awful words, but how else can I describe it? – heavy petting were all catching up with me and when I saw a taxi coming down the road with its orange light on, I made a snap decision and hailed it.

'Didn't you ask him back with you?' asked Jools.

'No. I thought it would look a bit keen. Anyway, he

lives in Kenton, for God's sake. Why didn't he invite me back?' I said indignantly.

'Maybe he shares a house with some other blokes. You know how men are . . . maybe he didn't want you to see his pad until he'd cleaned up all the remnants of several days' Indian takeaways from the living room. You know what I mean?'

'Hmmm.' It seemed pretty unlikely to me, but when you fancy someone, your imagination will stretch to virtually any unlikely excuse as to why they're not recipro-cating. I began to visualize trays of congealing chicken korma and felt strangely reassured.

'I bet he'll call tonight. It's like they *know* when you're not thinking about them any more, and they can't *bear* it.'

I was dubious.

'He's too young for me anyway,' I said with finality.

'Don't be daft.'

'No, he is. He's really very immature,' I said.

'That's got nothing to do with age,' said Jools, 'where men are concerned.'

'You're right. You should have heard Martin this morning . . .'

'This is your boss who is your friend but you're not bonking but everyone thinks you are?'

'The very same. This morning I came in and the first thing he says is, "Will you be any use with your arm in a sling?" I said to him, "Shall we start that again? You're meant to say, 'Soph, how good of you to come into work when you're in such pain', and I'm meant to say, 'That's all right, boss, the typing may be a bit slower, but I'll struggle on.'" Instead, he's all grumpy because I left the wedding without saying goodbye – I was going to hos-pital, for Christ's sake – which is so hypocritical, because if he'd managed to get his tongue down Arnie's daughter's throat, he wouldn't have thought about saying goodbye to me either . . .'

'That's not immaturity, that's jealousy,' Jools observed. 'Are you sure he doesn't fancy you?'

'Quite sure,' I said, although I had caught Martin looking at me rather oddly when Dave and I returned from the garden to see Mum and Reg 'go away'.

I had realized, catching a glimpse of my dishevelled self in the hall mirror in the hotel lobby that it was pretty obvious what Dave and I had just been doing. It wasn't so much that my dress was extremely crumpled at the back and had grass stains where the material had been ground into the lawn, nor that there were love bites on my neck (I have very pale skin and even a slightly overenthusiastic kiss leaves a mark), it was more that my body was kind of glowing with sexual anticipation. Unsatisfied sexual anticipation, as it turned out.

I dismissed the thought that I was the object of Martin's unrequited passion. Men just weren't like that, were they? Surely if they knew what it felt like, they wouldn't make women suffer in the way that they do.

Jools thought this was a typically female argument.

Martin was at a planning meeting with all the other vice-presidents of the bank. I spent most of the afternoon on the phone to Dan. He was in New York for his American publication and he was at a loose end. He said he was ringing to invite me to his publication party at the Groucho Club in a couple of weeks' time, but I sensed he wanted to chat, so I rang him back at his hotel and asked him what the problem was. Apparently he and Donny, his lover of many years, were going through a bad patch.

79

'He says he's sick of people dying in my books. In the first, the main character's lover commits suicide, and in this one the main character's lover has Aids. Donny thinks I'm subconsciously trying to get rid of him. It's so typical of Donny to think that everything anyone does revolves around him. Enough of our friends have died for me to know what it's like, for heaven's sake.'

'Well, the character is nothing like Donny anyway,' I said.

'Will you tell him that, Soph? He'd believe it from you. Honestly, he's making such a fuss. It's making life very difficult.'

'Perhaps he's having trouble dealing with your success.'

Until his first novel sold for a huge amount of money in America, Dan had been the quieter one of the couple. Donny was always much louder and ostensibly successful. Now, with the recession, Donny's very eighties interior-design business was struggling, and although he was trying to adjust stylistically (stocking real Connecticut whitewash, for instance, and importing Madras cotton checks to replace the swags and tails he had been so fond of), I thought that he must be suffering financially.

As well as that, I thought, there must always be the spectre of HIV, which Dan had written about so eloquently. Even though we had all been friends since the first year at university, I had never known, or wanted to know, whether Donny and Dan were faithful to one another. They had always been by far the most stable couple I knew, and I suppose I wanted to believe that two people could find one another completely satisfying. But I couldn't help myself asking, with more than formulaic politeness, whenever we spoke these days, how they were, and I sometimes found myself checking them over when we met to reassure myself that there hadn't been any drastic weight loss.

'Are you all right otherwise?' I asked.

'Very well,' said Dan. 'Both books have sold in Germany now, and Japan, of all places. You don't know anyone who speaks Japanese, do you?'

'Yes, but not well enough to translate,' I said.

'No, I didn't mean that. It's just that I can't see how a gay love story set in Glasgow is going to go down in Tokyo, can you? I just wanted someone to be able to read it and reassure me that my characters haven't changed sex, or whatever.'

'But you don't speak any other languages, do you,' I remarked, 'so how are you ever going to know?'

'I suppose I feel OK when there's a recognizable script. It's just those characters and starting at the back of the book that worry me.'

We prattled on for a while, until I glanced out of my office and noticed Pat staring at me from the other side of the room. She quickly flicked her eyes out of focus, as if she hadn't been watching me at all, but couldn't resist a glance at the clocks.

She did have a point. It was four o'clock and I had successfully managed to fill the day doing practically nothing. Now I turned on my computer and doodled guiltily with one hand in the Paintbrush facility. It was more fun than playing solitaire and, if anyone was checking, it was less obvious that I was unoccupied.

At five-thirty I switched off my computer, neglecting to save my doodles, turned out the light in Martin's office and was just about to leave, when the phone rang.

'Hallo?' I had long since dropped answering the phone as Martin Young's secretary, since most of the phone calls seemed to be for me.

81

'Hallo, Sophie. How are you getting along?' said a familiar voice.

These days, whenever she rang, I tried to envisage what my mystery caller looked like. It was difficult to create a full picture because we normally exchanged only a few words. Her voice was fairly ordinary. It didn't have a distinctive London twang. There was a hint of a country accent lingering somewhere around the vowels, but I couldn't place it. Generally the voice was flat – like a bored bank teller, or someone who rings up to sell you double-glazing – but sometimes she let the seriousness drop, almost taking herself by surprise, and a nervous laugh would escape.

It was not a young voice, but it wasn't an old one either. I pictured her as middle-aged, with a short, easy-to-care-for perm. I always saw her from behind, and when I had once turned her round to face me, her face was just a blur. Sometimes I imagined her sitting at a desk, sometimes she was standing in the hall of a small terraced house. Today I visualized her in a phone box (there was a lot of noise in the background, as if there were heavy traffic nearby). There were shopping bags on the floor beside her. She was wearing a knee-length skirt in turquoise and a beige cardigan, an outfit that did nothing to disguise her rather lumpy figure. She was trying to ignore the collage of business cards stuck to the wall in front of her. Messages such as SEX SLAVE and TV MASSAGE printed on coloured paper with crude illustrations surrounded the list of international dialling codes above the telephone. I didn't think that she would approve. I realized I was imagining someone very like Reg's sister, who played a lot of bridge and spent spare moments trawling the local supermarkets around closing time for cut-price fondant fancies.

'Fine, thanks,' I said, jerking myself out of my reverie. 'How are you?'

'I'm fine,' she said and giggled.

I decided to be bold.

'Listen, do I know you?' I asked in what I thought was a light, unthreatening tone.

I could sense the hesitation. I could almost hear through the silence her mental deliberation about answering.

'In a way,' she said, 'I think you do,' then added quickly, 'I've got to go now.'

I had detected a pattern to the calls. There was usually one around eleven in the morning, then one just before lunch. Often she called as I was about to leave the office. Sometimes, if I asked a question, or sounded annoyed, she would immediately hang up the phone and wouldn't call again for several days. There was nearly always a call on Monday. It was as if she had spent the weekend working up to ringing.

I picked up my handbag and walked towards the lifts, deep in thought.

I could see Dawn, the receptionist, tidying her desk as the glass lift slid towards the ground floor. She flicked the switchboard on to nightline and gathered up her things. Perhaps it was the mousy perm, or the plastic carrier bag from Tesco that I could see by her side behind the desk, that fitted in so nicely with my fantasy. I was suddenly convinced that she was a very logical suspect.

Maybe she had created some kind of bizarre distraction to entertain herself when she got bored. The only problem with this theory was that since she seemed to find it so much of an effort to put on a civil voice to me at the best of times, it seemed peculiar that the anonymous calls were always so friendly. But perhaps that was just to put me off the scent. In the split second between the lift reaching its destination and the doors opening, I decided to confront her.

'Any idea who keeps calling me?' I asked, as casually as I could.

'What do you mean?' I thought she sounded defensive.

'You know. There's a woman who keeps calling me. Mainly around lunchtime and in the evenings. You put a call through about five minutes ago,' I said, leaning forward and resting my elbows on her desk.

'Oh, *her*. I always think it's your mother,' said Dawn. 'I mean, who else would call so often? She's nervous, doesn't like the telephone, like a lot of older people, and she always asks for Sophie Fitt, not Martin Young's secretary.'

For someone normally so laconic, I thought she was being suspiciously voluble. I realized it had been a stupid move to talk to her, since she was hardly likely to let on if she had been making the calls herself.

'You mean you don't know who it is?' she said, as if finally realizing the implication of my question. 'Spooky.'

Chapter Eleven

I was surprised, and rather pleased, to see that the publican had broadened the base of his advertising campaign. There were several copies of my poster fly-posted on bus shelters along the Essex Road. The production quality was crude. I suspected that the photocopier he had used was running out of toner, but I quite liked the effect, thinking that it made me look like the lead singer in an all-girl punk band.

I wasn't on until after the interval, so I sat at the bar surveying the crowd. Janine, the Australian barmaid, brought me a glass of mineral water and said that she was looking forward to my act. There weren't enough female comedians, and she was sick of jokes about the World Cup.

'Oh!' she cried, suddenly remembering something. 'There was an envelope for you under the door this morning when I opened up. I forgot.'

She was in the middle of pouring a couple of pints and when she had taken the money, she came back from the till with the customer's change as well as a lilac envelope for me.

My name c/o the pub was written in childish round handwriting. The card was a bit twee, with a cute hedgehog poking its snout through a horseshoe. Inside, in the same handwriting, was the message 'BREAK A LEG!'

'Charming,' said Janine, when I showed it to her. 'As

if you haven't got enough broken limbs to cope with,' she said, pointing at my sling. 'Still, it's traditional on the stage, isn't it?'

'Did your mother ever tell you that Sex is the Price that Women Pay for Marriage and Marriage is the Price that Men Pay for Sex? . . . She did? . . . You remember how she said it? . . . You do? A bit wearily, as if she knew all about that, thank-you-very-much. You really got the message, right, and you started off your teenage years pushing boys' hands away from your breasts and thinking that they were ONLY AFTER ONE THING, d'you remember? Then someone tells you, some older girl at school, usually, a bit of a slag, actually, but you're quite chuffed that she's bothering to speak to you . . . anyway, she says something one day while she's lipsticking up in the toilets that makes you realize that you're meant to LIKE having your breasts touched. And you suddenly realize that boys aren't just doing it thinking that they can go ALL THE WAY with you, they're actually doing it to TURN YOU ON. God, you feel a fool. No wonder Mark in the fourth form didn't want to walk you home after drama group again. God, you must have seemed like an ungrateful little cow. Next time, thanks to your MORE EXPERIENCED friend in the fifth form, you'll be COOL. So . . . next time comes along and Pete, who you REALLY FANCY, even despite his skin problem, slides his hand up your angora sweater in the flicks, you kind of sigh, to kind of show him that you like it, without saying anything, like, because Robert Redford's being a bit reflective on screen and it's a bit quiet. Pete thinks that you're telling him to stop, so he presses a bit harder, and you start breathing a bit quickly, kind of trying to make it a bit obvious that you

REALLY DO LIKE THAT. So Pete whispers "Are you OK?", and you say "Yeaher . . . " And as soon as Pete hears that he stops . . . And what you don't realize then, as you're sitting in the back row with one tit hanging over the top of your teen bra, thinking that you must have done something wrong because Pete's hands are now firmly in his own lap, is that this is only the beginning of a lifetime of non-communication with men.

'Still in store for you are endless wonderings whether you seemed TOO KEEN, endless debating why he SAID he would phone if he didn't MEAN it. And yes, your telephone line is just fine. There's the dialling tone when you pick it up to check for the tenth time, and, yes, your answerphone is working, and let's face it, it is PRETTY UNLIKELY that he lost that piece of paper with your number on it. And NO, he DIDN'T leave it in the back pocket of his jeans when he took them round to do a service wash. And NO, you really can't ring him, even if YOU JUST WANT TO KNOW WHERE YOU STAND, particularly if you just want to know where you stand, because that's PRESSURE, and you know what men think about THAT.

'When he does ring, of course, or if, you're in such a state that you BLOW IT AGAIN. First of all, you're INCREDIBLY COOL and nonchalant, because he's obviously a bastard because he didn't ring . . . But hang on a minute! Something wrong in that analysis, because he's on the phone now. Better late than never, you think, so you ask him a bit sarcastically if he's been away, and he's mystified. So you try to cover your tracks. You've been pretty busy yourself, you say, although when he asks you what you've been up to, the best you can come up with is "Oh . . . this and that." This is when you realize that you've been a complete moron. He has called,

87

hasn't he? He never said WHEN he was going to call, did he? So suddenly you're really nice and giggly and charming, which is when he makes some excuse and rings off.

'You're approaching thirty, for God's sake, but you're still the optimistic, sexually awakening fourth-former in the back row of the local Odeon.

'And you go through all this just for a FUCK.

'Which just goes to show that your mother was wrong. The price women pay for sex is this: HOURS AND HOURS OF WAITING FOR THE PHONE TO RING, DAYS OF SELF-DOUBT, WEEKS OF STARVING YOURSELF, BECAUSE HE PROB-ABLY THOUGHT YOU LOOKED BETTER WITH YOUR CLOTHES ON, AND A HUGE ACCESS BILL FOR CRATES OF AUSTRALIAN WHITE WHINING WITH YOUR BEST FRIEND. And Mum, forget marriage, the price of sex for men is TWO MINUTES' CHEAP RATE ON THE MOBILE PHONE . . . Thank you. Good-night.'

The reception was mixed. An all-women crowd who were knocking back bottles of Chardonnay right in front of me obviously identified with the last monologue, but it seemed to have passed most of the audience by. I sensed that I should have stuck with my made-up characters, rather than talking, in a thinly disguised way, about myself. I had enjoyed it, however, even if no one else had.

I discovered, when I took my bow, that, having given my frustrations a voice, I was feeling unburdened. It crossed my mind that I may have inadvertently hit upon a new form of therapy. I decided to discuss it with my friend Stephanie, who is an expert on all things alternative, from colour auras to colonic irrigation, when we next met. Maybe she and I could contrive one of those weekend workshops she was always paying thousands of pounds to participate in. We could call it something like 'Stand up ... to your fears' and people could pay us huge amounts of money to stand up in front of a pub audience and joke about their insecurities.

I took another bow and gathered together my props.

The part of the show that had got the most laughs, in particular from someone at the back whom I couldn't see but could hear almost choking on a fit of giggles, was, as usual, Something Funny, who this week had been at the annual office party.

With her hand poised above an imaginary tray of finger food, Something Funny started to detail the dangers lurking among the hors-d'oeuvres. She warned of killer canapés and gave extensive descriptions of the bacterial content of dip. Not everyone was fatally allergic to peanuts, she granted, but it would take a strong constitution to stand up to the dose of diarrhoea that would follow indulgence in the spinach and goat's-cheese roulade. The barbecue colouring on the crisps might well lead to hyperactivity and one couldn't be sure that the quail's eggs had spent long enough in boiling water without biting into them, and then ... well, it might just be too late. At least, she said, bringing a familiar blue packet out of her capacious handbag, you knew where you were with a rich tea.

This monologue had been inspired by a tabloid headline I had spotted in the week that read: 'CELEBRITIES IN PÂTÉ PANIC'.

Because of the hot weather, the newspapers were filled with food-poisoning horror stories. It had got to the point where you almost expected a bravery award for eating a kebab. The punters were obviously as fed up with it as I was.

I had been intending to drop Something Funny, or at least give her a rest, because I was getting a bit bored. (Also, there had been a couple of occasions recently when I had found myself thinking, and even sounding, like her when I wasn't on the stage.) But I decided that she would have to continue for the time being, if she remained this popular.

As I pulled on a fresh T-shirt, I started to think about her theme for the next Saturday. I wondered how Something Funny would react to receiving a spate of anonymous phone calls. Then I remembered the card that Janine had given me. I pulled it out of my bag and read it again. Obviously it was from a fan who didn't want me to know their name. There was no reason to suppose that it emanated from the same source as the phone calls, except that it too was anonymous. And oddly friendly. And the handwriting looked like a woman's. I put the card away.

I had no real idea of what Mars was fond of calling the *profile* of my audience, except that they were mostly youngish. Sometimes I thought I recognized a face or two; occasionally someone would congratulate me at the bar, or buy me a drink; there were often other comedians around. Sometimes a friend would turn up – I could always tell when Donny and Dan were in the audience, because Donny had the embarrassing habit of shouting '*Brava!*' at every pause, as if he were at the opera – but most of them had better things to do on a Saturday evening. Sometimes I had better things to do on a Saturday evening too, so I tried to get on before the interval, and I usually didn't hang around to do market research.

For a few weeks after the Edinburgh Festival the year before, where I had been very well received on the Fringe, I had attempted half-heartedly to do a bit more networking with fellow players, hoping perhaps to be included on a late-night improvisation show on Channel 4, or some such. But I'm not a natural schmoozer and as my plans to live in Europe took shape, I soon had an excuse to stop making the effort.

Since those plans had been scuppered, I thought as I wiped off some mascara that had run beneath my lower lashes, and since the publican was at last making some effort to promote me, maybe I should hang around this evening and see who was in.

'I'm sorry I didn't call,' said a voice behind me. I spun round.

Dave had poked his face round the curtain and was smiling cheekily at me.

'I've been on late shifts all week, you see,' he said and thrust a hand holding a bunch of wilting freesias towards me.

'Oh, thanks. I didn't really expect you to call,' I said, sounding as distant as I could.

'That's not what it sounded like out there,' said Dave.

'What? You didn't think . . . ' I started, but I could feel a blush creeping up all over my face and decided to leave it at that. 'Look, I don't think you should be here anyway. This bit is for performers only,' I said.

'OK. OK! I'll see you out the front. What are you drinking?'

We drank quite a lot of lager and as we were passing through Camden in a cab, Dave spotted an Indian restaurant and insisted we go for the inevitable late-night Saturday curry. While Dave was paying the fare, another taxi drew up behind us. The person in the back seemed to be having a discussion with the driver. The driver kept turning round to the passenger, then turning back huffily and looking at me. Dave looked round and we walked into the restaurant. The waiter showed us to a table in the window and handed us menus. As we sat down, I saw the taxi was still there. In my efforts to see the passenger, I misjudged the space between my forehead and the window.

'Ow!'

'What are you staring at?' asked Dave, looking up.

'I think we've been followed,' I said. 'No, don't look ... OK, look now. They're driving away. Did you see anything?'

'Which car are you talking about?'

'The taxi, of course.'

'Oh, I wasn't looking at the taxi. I thought you meant the red Toyota.'

'Oh, honestly!' I said, quite annoyed. 'If John Thaw ever wants a new sidekick, don't bother to apply for the job.'

'Sorry,' said Dave. 'What on earth makes you think they were following us, anyway?'

'Well, some people would say it's because I've got an overactive imagination,' I said, thinking of Martin. 'Look, you know I was telling you about those strange phone calls at work? Well, tonight I got this at the pub.'

I pulled the card out of my large leather satchel.

'Ugh,' said Dave, looking at the picture. 'That's horrible.' Then he looked inside at the message. 'I don't understand.'

'Nor do I. That's the whole point,' I said.

I tried to explain, but the more I tried to grasp at the truth, the more elusive it became. Dave pretended to be concentrating for a while, as he broke off bits of poppadom and munched them thoughtfully, but his eyes were glazing over and I could tell that he was becoming as confused as I was.

'I certainly didn't see the receptionist in the audience, anyway,' I said, pausing for breath.

A couple of seconds passed before Dave realized that a response was probably required.

'Did she say she'd come?' he ventured.

'Oh, you haven't been listening! Well, maybe it isn't the receptionist after all. Maybe she was telling the truth. Or, maybe . . . ' I continued for my own benefit, since I had completely lost Dave now, 'maybe that's exactly what she wants me to think, and she's putting me off the track since I confronted her.' In an advanced state of inebriation, that sounded plausible for a moment. But I was sure I had never mentioned my stand-up routine to her and she didn't seem like the sort of person who would scour the small print of the *Time Out* comedy section. No, whichever way I looked at it, the person who rang had not sent the card. Which seemed to simplify things, except that it meant I had now attracted the attention of two unknown people. Perhaps my fan had been in the audience. I was glad that I hadn't thought of this before I went on. I didn't like the idea of someone in the audience watching me, so to speak, let alone following me to a tandoori restaurant in Camden. I was quite relieved we had decided to stop the taxi before we got to my flat.

'What I don't understand is why somebody wants you to hurt yourself . . . ' Dave was clearly several steps back and still looking at the greetings card.

93

I tried to explain that 'break a leg' wasn't as nasty as it sounded in the theatre.

'A broken leg can be pretty nasty wherever it happens,' he said. 'Perhaps you just mean a stress fracture.'

'No, no,' I said, trying to get the conversation back to metaphor from medicine. 'It's a superstition . . . like not talking about the Shakespeare play about the Scottish king . . .'

'Which one's that, then?' Dave had a half-gallon-of-lager look about him.

'I'll tell you in the morning,' I said, and, finding I couldn't really focus on the menu, ordered myself a chicken biryani, which was the easiest thing to eat with one hand.

When I eventually gave Dave a full account of my mystery phone calls after several glasses of freshly squeezed orange juice and four black coffees on Sunday morning, he was much more concerned than I had expected. I suppose I am used to Martin's boringly logical dismissal of my conspiracy theories, so I may have slightly overestimated the number of anonymous phone calls I had received, and I may have exaggerated, just a touch, the spookiness of my caller's voice.

'Sounds like *Misery*,' said Dave.

'Actually, I think I'm keeping rather cheerful, in the circumstances,' I said proudly.

'No, I meant the book, by Stephen King. He's my favourite author. It was a film too. Didn't you see it?'

I have never read a horror novel in my life, and when Dave started telling me the story of Annie Wilkes in graphic detail, I realized why.

I found myself backtracking.

'Well, when I say dozens of phone calls every week,

perhaps I just meant half a dozen. And, I mean, this person obviously doesn't mean me any harm. OK, OK, I know that the woman in the novel was a fan too, but that's fiction, right, not real life, and there's no evidence that it's the same person, anyway . . . Yes, I am sure we weren't being followed last night . . . I mean, there were hundreds of taxis drawing up in Camden.'

'Do you know, you're really cute when you're chattering away,' Dave interrupted. 'But shut up a minute and come here.'

I was sitting cross-legged at the bottom of the bed. I clambered towards him.

'Let's take a look at this arm,' he said, removing the sling. He gently manipulated it, twisting it one way and then the other. It was much less painful than it had been the week before.

'I don't think you need to wear that any more,' he pronounced, throwing the sling on the floor.

Then he started unbuttoning the thin white cotton nightie I was wearing.

'I'm not sure you need to wear this either,' he said, smiling.

I suppose that dealing with other people's bodies all day gets rid of your inhibitions. I learned that Sunday why most of the heterosexual men I knew made a beeline for nurses at parties. I wouldn't say that Dave's lovemaking was clinical, but he certainly knew all about anatomy.

He had to leave very early on Monday morning. I stretched out in bed, exhausted but unable to sleep. My body felt as if it had been under anaesthetic for months but was now coming round. I felt in contact with every pore and every sinew, and I couldn't stop my facial muscles lifting into one big self-satisfied grin.

I decided to go for a run in the park. There was a slight dampness in the air as the sun was not yet hot enough to burn off the night's dew. Every flowerbed seemed to dance with pink, purple and red plants as I jogged past. I ran as far as the rose garden in the Inner Circle, where I paused to catch my breath and to inhale the sweet, sensual scent of my favourite deep-red roses. Then I walked back home, passing several other early-morning runners, feeling elated.

I stripped off my running shorts and T-shirt, and took them, along with the rest of my dirty washing, downstairs to the launderette, on my way out to work.

Elena was Sellotaping a handwritten notice to the inside of the window. It said 'Flat to let. Inquire within.'

'Does that mean that the underpinning is nearly finished?' I asked. Costas and his wife, Elena, had been waiting for the workmen to leave before putting the flat below mine on the market.

'Yeah. They say this week,' she replied.

She took my bag of washing and emptied it into a machine, looking at me curiously. I wouldn't say that Elena is nosy, but she doesn't miss much.

'So why you look like the cat got the cream?' she asked.

I smiled a bit coyly.

'Ah, yes, Costas said he thought there was a new boy.'

'But I haven't seen Costas for ages!'

'Yes, but he got big ears,' said Elena, and we both laughed.

Chapter Twelve

The envelope was pastel pink and I knew almost before I turned it over that the handwriting would be familiar. The card had a picture of a fluffy anthropomorphic hedgehog holding a cake with candles. Inside it said, simply, HAPPY BIRTHDAY. It was an innocuous, if tasteless, card bearing an innocuous message, but we were in the middle of a boiling-hot July and my birthday is in January.

I looked at the envelope. It had a W1 postmark. So, I deduced, it must be from one of the 4 million people who live or work in the metropolitan area. My shudder had nothing to do with the icy temperature of the air-conditioning.

Martin was already in. I walked into his office and showed him the birthday card.

'The hedgehog looks a bit spineless,' he joked weakly, then, looking up at my serious face, he added, 'Look, I'm really sorry. I forgot. I'll buy you lunch to make up for it.'

I laughed, breaking the tension.

'God, I must be a real harridan when I'm angry! You look positively chastened. Don't worry. You haven't done anything wrong. It's not my birthday, you see.'

'But why . . .?'

'You may well ask. Look, I know you'll think that I'm mad,' I said, 'but just listen. I think I'm being watched.'

I started to tell him about the feeling of being followed

on Saturday, the good-luck card at the pub, the nuisance calls.

'What do you mean nuisance calls?' Martin interrupted. 'I thought I'd put a stop to those. I spoke to Marie weeks ago.'

'Well, it wasn't Marie, as it turned out,' I said a bit sheepishly, because I hadn't ever got round to informing Martin. I explained that as soon as I had met Marie, I knew it couldn't be her, because of her accent. I told him my new suspicions about the receptionist.

'Well, thanks for filling me in before,' said Martin sarcastically. 'Marie must think I'm the one who's crazy.'

'So, you're saying I'm crazy, are you?' I said, my voice rising.

'All I'm saying is that you can't go round accusing everyone without having any evidence.'

'Well, I don't intend to, that's why I'm talking to you,' I said, conveniently forgetting to mention my conversation with Dawn on Friday. I hadn't exactly accused her, after all.

'What makes you think it has anything to do with working here, anyway?' Martin asked.

'Well, it's probably something to do with the fact that until I set foot in this building, I've never been pestered by anonymous phone calls and greetings cards before,' I replied, mimicking his patronizing tone.

'Don't you think you're being a bit paranoid?' said Martin calmly.

'Didn't you say that once before?' I said, referring to Martin's previous refusal to believe my theory about my first boss being murdered. Martin knew immediately what I was talking about.

'You were proved wrong there too,' he interrupted.

98

'That's not true,' I said. 'The man might not have been found guilty, but that doesn't mean he didn't do it.'

'It does in English law,' said Martin.

'God, you're pompous sometimes,' I said and walked out of his office.

Later he came over and put his hand on my shoulder.

'I'm sorry, Soph. You're right. There is something funny about getting a birthday card six months after the day. Even I'm never that late. Let me know if anything else happens. OK?'

I nodded silently.

I jumped every time the phone rang that day, but there was someone on the other end of the line each time I gingerly picked up the receiver.

'No funny calls today,' said the receptionist as I left the building. And for the first time since I had known her, she smiled.

Chapter Thirteen

Whenever I spoke to Martin about my worries, they seemed to go away, for a while. The phone calls at work suddenly stopped. By the end of the week, I was almost beginning to miss them. There were no cards or messages for me at the pub on Saturday. I did a monologue about getting anonymous phone calls in Something Funny's voice, and speaking my own thoughts in her wearying, worrying voice was a salutary lesson in the danger of letting things get out of proportion.

The publican informed me that for the next two Saturdays he was organizing an Edinburgh Festival preview, and since I wasn't going to Edinburgh this year, he wasn't including me. I made a mental note not to do him any favours in future.

On Sunday I was woken from a rather hot and bothered dream by the smell of burning and my name being shouted from the little patio behind the launderette downstairs.

Flustered and still half asleep, I pulled the top sheet off the bed and looked around the room, wondering what to attach it to. I vaguely remembered hearing that people had saved themselves from fires by knotting their sheets together and letting themselves down to safety slowly, rather than leaping out of high windows. Unable to find a suitable fixture, I wrapped the sheet around me, sarong-style, and peeped out of my bedroom window.

Costas, my landlord and the owner of the launderette, was gesticulating wildly with what looked like a couple of long pokers. Flames leapt from behind him.

'Sophie! We have barbecue! We celebrate the end of builders. You join us!'

'Now?' A quick glance at my alarm clock had told me that it was only ten o'clock in the morning. I like souvlaki, but not for breakfast.

'No. I just heat the coals. Lunch. OK?'

'OK,' I said and flopped back on to the bed, but I found I couldn't get back to sleep.

I decided to ring Dave. He had been on late shift all week. He had called once to say how much he had enjoyed himself last weekend, and he had said that he would phone when his shift pattern changed. But he hadn't, and I assumed he wouldn't. Maybe I had been too clinging, I thought. Maybe he had thought I was wanting more commitment. Men hate the 'c' words – clinging, cuddle, commitment. I had been so distracted by my mystery caller, I couldn't work out whether I cared (another 'c' word men aren't keen on) or not.

He was just in from his shift. He sounded tired. I tried to effect a cheerful don't-care-if-you-do, don't-care-if-you-don't voice, and asked him if he would like to come over for a barbecue. He said, in his jokey way, that he had just been dealing with some third-degree burns and that charred flesh was about the last thing he could face at the moment, so, if I didn't mind, he'd take a rain check. I took the hint and rang off quickly.

I went downstairs and asked Costas if there was anything I could bring to the party. Surprisingly he said yes, a large tomato salad, if I didn't mind. Of course I did mind. I had been thinking in terms of red or white, but I could hardly say that to him since I was the one who'd asked.

As I made my way to Camden Sainsbury's, I felt charitable enough, thinking that Costas must have forgotten that I didn't possess a car, but as I struggled back through the grungy crowds of Camden Lock, with three enormous carrier bags, scanning the traffic fruitlessly for the golden light of a free taxi, I wasn't in the best of party moods. (Why is it that you can never leave the supermarket carrying only the item you intended to buy? Is there something sinister in the design of the place that impels you to buy nets of oranges and attractively packaged blueberries, quantities of mixed green and purple lettuce leaves and fresh herbs that you will sadly scrape out of your salad cool-tray a month later, a yellowing slime of their former selves?)

I changed into a man's dress shirt with a wing collar and tails that I had found in the Hampstead Oxfam shop. Over a pair of black and white striped leggings, it looked quite smart, and, more importantly, covered the slight wave in the stripes that occurred about two inches below the hips. Since the party was only downstairs I decided to go barefoot. I was rather proud of the fact that, under the influence of the meticulously groomed Jools, I had painted my toenails for the first time in my life. The colour was Tulip Pink and I had lipstick to match. I clipped on some large plastic earrings in the same colour. I looked in my cheval mirror and decided that I looked like a liquorice allsort. Eat your heart out, Dave, I thought, in a mood to flirt with the first man I came across.

There was an incongruous sign on the door of the launderette saying 'Closed for Private Party'. Some of the guests, who had spilled out of the tiny rooms at the back where Costas and Elena live, were sitting on the washing machines chatting. I recognized most of the faces.

Over the past few years a number of Costas's relations have moved into the area, and since I've been the only person rash enough to buy one of the flats above the launderette, I am treated as an honorary family member at the taverna down the road and get special rates at the dry-cleaners.

Costas's concern for my single status is legendary and I have lost count of the number of bottles of retsina I have downed with cousins of his in the hope of finding true love. The only man Costas has seen me with is Martin and he is mystified that our relationship is purely platonic. He smiles knowingly, alarmingly like my mother, when the subject is raised. Once he said that no man could be friends with me without wanting to sleep with me, which I found rather flattering (politically incorrect, I know, but what the hell), until I heard him talking to the bartender at the taverna over an ouzo or two one evening when I was having dinner there with Donny and Dan.

'No man is friend with any woman, even if she ugly, without trying to fuck her' were his exact words, and since the taverna was unusually empty, they echoed round the room, followed by my giggles as Donny said in his campest voice, 'How long have we all been friends, Soph? Can you *imagine* how frustrated I've been?'

I gently pushed my way through the crowd round the giant spin-dryer, wishing that I had had the presence of mind to put cling film on the large plate of tomato salad I had made.

'Mmmm, delicious,' said a man I didn't recognize, putting his finger into the dressing and licking.

So it should be, I thought. Determined to do things right, I had bought the best ingredients I could find for the dressing and had spent over £10 on pretty bottles of olive oil and balsamic vinegar, the remains of which I just knew would gather dust on the shelves in my kitchen until I finally decided to throw them out.

'What's this herb?'

'It's chervil. They had run out of basil,' I said.

'It's an interesting change.'

Perhaps the chervil was a mistake. These days I find that interesting is practically always a euphemism for nasty, whether it's food or people being described.

I wondered how it was that some people, when faced with the wrong ingredients for a recipe, managed to create something delicious. Caesar, for instance, whoever he was, must once have looked in his cupboard and said, 'Mmmm, a tin of anchovies and a raw egg, I'm sure I can make a delicious salad with that.' If it had been me, a forgettable dish called Very Salty Egg Scrambled in Fishy Oil would have emerged.

I looked around for somewhere to dump the salad. Costas's fat cousin George, who often tries to woo me with the honey-dripping pastries he bakes, caught my eye and started to push his way over to me. I was glad that my new-found foodie friend seemed determined to continue our conversation. Being considerably taller than me, he managed to clear a path to the patio, where I put down the plate on a large trestle table which was covered in blue and white checked tablecloths from the taverna.

'Oh, fuck!' I said, looking down at my shirt, which now had an oily brown line of salad dressing across the front at tummy level.

'I couldn't help noticing a washing machine in the front room,' said my companion, rather wittily.

I smiled up at him and, now that I was less flustered, took a good look at his face. Apart from a rather pronounced receding hairline (in a less desperate mood I would have said bald), he had an attractive, intelligent face.

'Hallo,' I said, holding out my hand. 'Sophie Fitt.'

'Jonathan Stone,' he replied. 'I'm delighted to meet you at last.'

He made it sound as if he had been searching for me all his life.

'What do you do?' we both said at once and laughed self-mockingly.

'Very north London,' I said. 'I hate the idea that one's career is the most important thing, but it's always the first question I seem to ask too. I'll go first. Depending on who I'm with I'm a banker, or a secretary, or a comedienne.'

'A comedienne?'

I have found I can tell quite a lot about a man by giving him a choice of professions. The ones who say 'Oh, a banker?' are generally going to be pretty driven and competitive, the ones who say 'A secretary?' usually have some kind of problem with powerful women, but at least they pay for dinner. I tend to like the ones who say 'A comedienne?' best. We were off to a flying start.

'Well, I do a stand-up gig once in a while in Islington.'

'Oh, hang on a minute, you're not Miss Fitt, are you? Were you at Edinburgh last year?'

'Yes. I was actually.' This was getting better and better. A man with an interest in the fringe. I wondered why Costas hadn't mentioned him to me before.

'So were we.'

'Oh? And who are "we"? I mean "you"?' I inquired.

'The Write On Co-operative. I'm an actor stroke director stroke playwright. I've just finished writing my first play.'

'How *fascinating*,' I said, with good Thespian false enthusiasm. My heart had already sunk. I knew Write On to be a highly regarded but rather worthy troupe with a kind of vegetarian philosophy to their performance. Perhaps it had been the tomato salad rather than my looks that had attracted him over to talk to me.

'What's your play about?' I felt obliged to ask.

'Oh, you know, relationships and sharing, that fine balance between commitment and oppression, you know . . .' He turned his palms upwards in a disingenuous display of modesty. 'You kind of have to be there . . .'

In other words, a wank. I was saved from having to express any further interest by the arrival of a rather raddled but nevertheless beautiful woman with cascades of dark, rippled hair who was wearing a cream Nicole Farhi jersey dress. She put her arm through his in quite a proprietorial way and dazzled me with a smile.

'Melanie. This is Sophie Fitt. My partner, Melanie.'

I couldn't help noticing that she was wearing a wide gold wedding ring. I think it is absurd to marry someone and then be afraid of using the words wife or husband. Either you believe in the institution or you don't.

'Jonathan was just telling me about his play,' I said. 'Are you involved too?'

'Of course,' she said, as if slightly taken aback. 'We share everything.'

People who use the word share a lot are, in my experience, particularly possessive and ungenerous.

'I'm surprised you haven't heard us rehearsing,' she added.

I looked perplexed.

'We're your neighbours. Oh, Jonathan, didn't you say?'

'But . . . I thought . . .' I thought that my neighbours were a nameless, downtrodden woman and her vicious boyfriend, Simon. I felt incredibly embarrassed, but equally determined not to show it.

'Oh, no,' I said, thinking quickly. 'I haven't heard a thing. I'm out a lot.'

'Sophie was at Edinburgh last year too. She's a comedienne,' said Jonathan.

'A comedienne,' Melanie repeated, with an amused smile. 'How *fascinating*! A comedienne who likes to sing torch songs in her bath . . .'

I presumed she was referring to my do-it-yourself karaoke sessions with my Patsy Cline's *Greatest Hits* CD. It had been a tough week.

I could tell that Melanie had disliked me on sight just as much as I had disliked her.

'Are you going to Edinburgh this year?' she inquired, but without waiting for an answer she added, looking at her watch, 'Darling, we really must be going. Dipak did say two o'clock.'

I assumed she was referring to a brilliant young Indian playwright who was being fêted all over London. He was one of the few people you could refer to by first name only in the certainty that others would understand both who you were talking about and that you were on intimate terms.

'We *must* get together some time,' said Jonathan as they departed.

'*Absolutely*,' I replied with equal sincerity.

Elena, seeing that I had been left momentarily adrift,

came over with a glass of wine, which I drank quickly. The whole encounter with the Stones had unnerved me and undermined my confidence in my judgement.

First of all, I had started flirting with a man who was transparently a prat, and, more importantly, I had created a scenario in my imagination about my neighbours (I had even discussed it with Jools, wanting another opinion about whether I should think of intervening) that was patently untrue on the basis of a few overheard sentences.

'She's ghastly, isn't she?'

I laughed with relief that Elena agreed with my assessment, and I was pleased to notice as we watched her departing that although Melanie was very slim, there was a definite visible panty-line ruining the line of her Nicole Farhi dress.

'Have you met Liz?' asked Elena, taking the arm of the woman who had sidled up next to her.

Elena is quite a robust woman who likes to dress in rich, stained-glass-window colours. Her thick black hair is strong, almost wiry, and she uses black kohl round her dark eyes, and dark, plum-coloured lipstick. She was wearing a cherry-red T-shirt and a long, full skirt made from an Indian bedspread, the sort that was just coming back into fashion, although I suspected that Elena had been wearing hers since its original purchase in the early seventies.

Next to her, Liz was so pale in her pastel-pink summer dress she looked almost translucent. She was a little taller than me, with a slight frame, and I thought at first that she was about my age, but her bare upper arms had that tell-tale fleshiness that seems to attach itself to women in their middle thirties. Her hair was shoulder-length and light brown. It looked as if it could do with a good two inches off to get it back into condition. Her face was pale, with no hint of make-up, but she had good, well-balanced features and when she smiled – a surprisingly wide, dimpled smile – her face lit up. Her eyes were grey and distinctly red-rimmed. I wondered whether she was suffering from hay fever.

'Hi, Liz,' I said.

'Liz has just moved into the flat below yours,' said Elena.

'Oh, welcome!' I said with more enthusiasm than I felt. After four years with no neighbours at all, I'd now met three in one afternoon. 'Not another actress, I hope?'

'Me?' Liz took a slight step back, as if she was unused to being addressed directly. With the pink dress and the pink eyes, she reminded me for a second of a frightened toy rabbit.

'Oh, no. I'm not an actress, no,' she said shyly.

'What do you do?' I asked.

'I work in a shop,' she replied.

'Really, which one?'

She named a large department store in Oxford Street.

'I think I smell burning. Would you excuse me?' said Elena, leaving us together as she went to help Costas calm down the barbecue.

Liz looked at me nervously and smiled. I smiled back.

'Are you new to the area?' I ventured.

'Yes.'

'It's my favourite bit of London,' I said. It was hard work extracting more than a monosyllable from her.

'Mine too, now,' she replied, adding, 'There's quite a lot to do, isn't there?'

'Is there? Like what?' Apart from eating and drinking, I couldn't think of anything at all to do in Primrose Hill.

One of the reasons I liked it so much was that, unlike Hampstead and Camden, the area wasn't invaded by tourists and shoppers every weekend.

'Well, there's the zoo. I've always wanted to go there . . .'

I had quite forgotten that the zoo was less than ten minutes' walk from my door, although I often heard the sea lions barking at feeding time. I had never been inside, even though I had lived in the area for several years.

'And it's much nearer the West End. I'm going to walk to work on nice days,' she continued, relaxing a little. 'I expect you find it's very convenient for the theatres, do you?'

'Uh, yes,' I said, trying to remember the last time I had been to a play, and feeling slightly guilty for consistently failing to take advantage of the attractions of living in London.

We chatted pleasantly enough for some time. Although we didn't really have much in common, I found her far more congenial company than my other neighbours, the Stones. She was quite easy to shock, but not prudish. It was refreshing to meet someone who seemed as untouched by cynicism, or sophistication, as she was. I felt she must have led quite a sheltered life. Rather gratifyingly, she found some of my tarter remarks outrageously funny. At one point she giggled almost hysterically, unintentionally attracting the attention of the whole room.

Towards the end of the afternoon, by which time there were only a few guests left, somebody happened to mention to Costas that there was a fair on Hampstead

Heath. He became as excited as a child and insisted that we all jump into taxis and go immediately.

I love everything about fairs – the lights, the rides, even that distinctive aroma of cheap gravy and frying onions – so I didn't take any persuading at all, but Liz was more reticent.

'Oh, no. I couldn't,' she said.

'Oh, come on!'

'No. I'm a real scaredy-cat. I daren't go on anything.'

'Oh, come on. If you don't come, I'll be the only girl, and quite honestly, I need protection from Costas's cousins.'

It was meant to be a joke, but Liz seemed to take me at my word.

'All right, then,' she said, quite seriously. 'I'll just get a cardigan from upstairs. And don't you think you'd better put something on your feet?'

I looked down at my bare pink toes, then followed her upstairs to get some plimsolls.

When I came back downstairs a few moments later, the door of her flat was ajar. I poked my head round.

'Liz?'

'I'm in here,' she called from the bathroom.

'Oh. I'll see you downstairs.'

'Come on in. I'll just be a minute. I'm taking out my lenses. They're new.'

So that was the explanation for her sore-looking eyes.

I followed her voice to the bathroom. The flat was very similar in layout to mine, although it had another bedroom where I had a roof terrace. Liz obviously hadn't unpacked her possessions yet because, unlike my flat, there was no mess lying around, giving the place personality. I was irrationally cross to see that her bathroom was furnished with a plain white suite and reasonably tasteful blue and white tiles with a pattern of shells. It seemed grossly unfair that someone who was only renting a flat should have a tolerable bathroom, whereas I, who had bought the flat from Costas, had to put up with a cut-price avocado number. It made me very aggressive towards him later on the dodgems.

As she had warned, Liz wasn't much fun at the fair. The only ride she dared go on was the old-fashioned carousel that had horses going up and down and played 'I'm Forever Blowing Bubbles' over and over again. I tried to entice her on to Paratroopers – umbrella seats that spun very fast and high and afforded fantastic views of London, if you dared open your eyes.

'Come on, it's no fun without someone to scream with,' I remonstrated.

'Honestly, I'd throw up,' said Liz.

'I'll come,' said Costas's cousin George.

'I expect you will. That's why I'm not going in the same seat as you,' I replied. It took Liz a couple of seconds to get it, but when she did she laughed so much that George even joined in and forgot about taking offence, as he usually did when I refused his advances or his syrupy cakes.

It was quite late by the time the group of us walked home together, eating candy floss and toffee apples. We all peered through the shining plate-glass windows into the darkened launderette. Apparently, Elena had cleared up all the debris from the party single-handed. Costas was all for continuing, but Liz and I urged him not to wake up Elena. So he tiptoed in alone and reappeared with a couple of bottles of Metaxa, and we traipsed up the stairs as quietly as we could to my flat.

Chapter Fourteen

Dear Sophie

I had been hoping that your interest in seeing me was just a passing one. There are a lot of things about being a father that I prefer not to think about, but I do remember clearly that even at the age of six you were a determined little girl, and, reading your recent letter, I see that nothing has changed. I am powerless to prevent us from meeting — especially since I grow more curious with each of your letters — but I must warn you that I think our meeting could only lead to disappointment on your part.

Thank you for telling me about Christine. I hope that this husband will make her happier than I managed to do. If she looks half as beautiful at her second wedding as she did at her first, he is a lucky creature.

I have not married again, although I have had a number of liaisons — dangereuses and recently more companionable and middle-aged. My present friend bears much of the responsibility for this garbled and hasty note.

There is a possibility of an exhibition in London next year. I think I may be able to persuade the gallery to fork out my fare, and if so, I shall endeavour to make contact then. If your financial situation improves, then do visit us in Paris. I'm afraid, although the spirit is enlivened by your letters, my purse is weak, and I am not able to help you with your costs.

As you already know, I have been an inadequate father to you, and I fear that I may not improve in your estimation.

Salut!

Marcus Fitt

I stood in the hall reading the letter. The envelope with its distinctive handwriting lying on the mat inside the communal front door, had resurrected a particularly vivid childhood memory of excitement that quickly dissipated as I read the text.

One minute my father seemed to be offering friendship, the next withdrawing it. It was a shame he had no money, but I had never asked to be subsidized in my prospective trip to France, and I was irritated that he had made it seem as if I had. I was broke, but I had always supported myself, and I resented the implication that I was expecting him to help out.

Then there was that phrase 'powerless to prevent us from meeting'. That sounded pretty negative. I was his daughter, for God's sake, not an assassin with a contract out on him. Inadequate father, I thought angrily, more like bloody hopeless!

At the same time I was intrigued. Who was this woman who had persuaded him to write to me? And where would his exhibition be? Why was the letter so short on detail? And why just '*Salut*'? Was 'Love' too much to ask after twenty-two years' absence? Two tears trickled down my cheeks.

'Bad news?' I hadn't heard Liz's door open, or her footfall on the stairs.

'Yes and no,' I said and wiped my eyes with the back of my hand. 'It's a bit complicated,' I sniffed.

'Have you had any breakfast?' asked Liz.

'No,' I said. 'I never do.'

'You should,' she said, adding, 'I'm going to have a coffee in the patisserie. I haven't had time to get myself sorted out yet, you see. D'you fancy joining me?'

I looked at my watch. It wouldn't matter if I was a bit late for work.

*

I scooped the chocolate froth off the top of my cappuccino and licked it off my spoon. I sometimes wonder how I managed in pre-cappuccino days. Coffee used to be something I avoided drinking out in London because it used to come from those stainless-steel jugs that sat on the hotplate all day, stewing the liquid until it tasted like watery creosote. For some unknown reason, one fine day in the late eighties, hundreds of tiny cappuccino outlets sprang up overnight on practically every London street, and it became virtually compulsory to drink it.

'That was fun yesterday, wasn't it?' I said.

'Yes,' said Liz, smiling broadly. 'It's so lovely being able to do what you want.'

'What do you mean?' I asked, surprised.

'Well, I was living with my mother before, and she's a bit strict – well, set in her ways, anyway,' said Liz.

So that's why she appeared so nervous and naïve. Liz had left home a lot later in life than most people.

'So you were living with your parents?' I asked.

'Well, my dad died recently,' said Liz, twisting a lock of hair round her finger.

'Oh, I am sorry,' I said.

'Don't worry,' she replied. 'It was quite a relief in a way.'

I assumed he had been suffering from a long illness. We both fell silent. Both thinking about our fathers. I clutched the letter in my jacket pocket. It felt reassuring. At least my father was alive.

'When did you leave home, then?' she asked me.

'More or less as soon as I got a job,' I said.

'You were in a bit of a hurry to get out, weren't you?' she asked.

'Not really,' I said. 'It was just more convenient for work. And I was used to living on my own after university.'

115

'Oh, you went to university, did you? Which one?' Liz asked.

'Cambridge,' I replied.

'Goodness, you must be very brainy. I expect your parents were ever so proud of you.'

I'd never really thought about it. An image of my mother in the new outfit she had bought for my graduation flitted across my mind. My father, in our brief correspondence, had not expressed any curiosity, let alone pride, in my achievements. My fingers crumpled the envelope in my pocket.

I asked if Liz had been to university. She giggled.

'Me? Oh, no! Far too stupid, me. Anyway, my father would never have allowed it. He liked to keep an eye on me.'

It sounded more like a Victorian childhood than a contemporary one.

'So, have you always worked in a shop?' I inquired.

'No,' she said wistfully. 'I was a nurse. I had to give it up, though. Health reasons.'

'My boyfriend's a nurse,' I said, feeling a bit silly about calling Dave a boyfriend, but it sounded ridiculous to say 'someone I went to bed with recently is a nurse'.

'Dave?' she said, finishing her coffee. 'I didn't know that. Come on. You don't want to be late for work.'

I walked towards the tube, slightly puzzled. I couldn't remember mentioning Dave by name. Liz walked off in the opposite direction to catch the 74 bus.

I had finally remembered to bring my newly laundered running shorts and T-shirt in to work, so it was quite a disappointment that Jools didn't ring to suggest meeting at lunchtime. I decided to go down to Eden anyway and brave a session of circuit-training.

It turned out that before being allowed to use the machines, I had to go through an instruction programme and, to my chagrin, I was given Fiammetta, a flame-haired dragon with a body like Madonna, who gave me a humiliating lecture about my strength-to-weight ratio, and counted me all the way up to twenty movements on each machine, when three seemed to me a more sensible number on my first day. I noticed that the blond male instructor, Kirk, was going a lot easier on his trainee, whom, after sneaking surreptitious glances at him in the walls of mirror, I finally recognized as the junior on the yen desk. In his suit I never would have suspected him of being hairy. I gave him a little wave from the bench press. I was rewarded with a clenched-teeth grimace, which I put down to the effort of the triceps machine.

My training session had taken so long, there was barely enough time to grab a plate of pasta salad in the restaurant.

I ate on my own, watching the committed swimmers doing serious lengths. Why, I wondered, is there always one man in every full pool who has to do an ostentatious splashy butterfly stroke?

As I was clearing my table, I heard a familiar raucous laugh emanating from a table almost hidden by foliage. I walked over.

Jools was sitting with a young guy with short hair who was wearing a nasty dark-green suit with a sheen on it, and a much older man dressed in an expensive, but slightly flashy, pale-grey suit. She looked up, the flicker of surprise on her face soon giving way to a gushing greeting.

'Sophie, you look great!'

'I've braved the circuit,' I said. 'Actually I'm exhausted.

I got Fiammetta . . .' I was about to say that she had missed her vocation as coach for the German team in the 1936 Olympics, when Jools interrupted me.

'Have you met Harry, who owns Eden?' she asked.

The grey suit got up. I shook his hand.

'And my colleague, Frank.' He remained seated, but smiled.

'Sophie's a . . .' I was sure that Jools was just about to give away the fact that I was a temp. I interrupted her.

'I'm late already,' I said apologetically. 'Nice to meet you all.'

I spent the afternoon on the phone to Dan. He seemed remarkably unphased by the fact that all the reviewers in England were tipping his novel for the Booker Prize.

'It's such a lottery,' he said, 'you just can't let it go to your head. Course I'm pleased if people like the book, but it's a bit nerve-racking, too. You know how the British are. As soon as they think that someone is getting beyond themselves, they start slagging them off. I wanted your advice, actually, Soph. I've got all this money, you see, and I'm about to get a whole lot more on the first day of filming . . .' Film rights in Dan's first novel had been sold to a director whose previous work had been pop videos. 'I was wondering . . .'

'Oh, Dan, I'm not the right person to ask about investments, you know. I can never quite believe that the stock exchange is so high, when industry is collapsing. I'm always expecting it to slump back to where it was in the seventies. That's why I never made much of a banker. It was all like Monopoly money to me.'

'That's not really what I meant,' said Dan. 'It's just that, you know, I have so much money and you don't have a lot, you know, and you have subsidence . . .'

'Thanks, Dan,' I interrupted him, 'but I'm fine, really. Give it to some deserving cause.'

'I can't think of a better one.'

'Dan, stop,' I said and changed the subject. It was very sweet of him to think of me, but on the whole our conversation was making me feel a bit of a failure.

I was beginning to realize that I couldn't go on as I was. If I wanted the freedom to pay off my debts and go abroad, I couldn't support the lifestyle that went along with a well-paid career, like nice clothes and meals and a flat in Primrose Hill.

On the way home I stopped outside the estate agent at the bottom of Regent's Park Road, and spent some time studying the details of similar properties. I calculated that my flat would now fetch about £20,000 less than I had paid for it in the mid-eighties, leaving me with negative equity, so even if I sold my flat, I wouldn't be entirely free from debt. This seemed like a very good reason not to sell it and I was filled with a perverse sense of relief. I love my flat and would find it very hard to leave.

I started calculating how much money I would really need to live on if I were strict with myself and didn't go out so much. As a start to my new regime I bought myself a boil-in-the-bag piece of frozen fish. But having saved on my evening meal, I immediately blew the rest of the £5 note on a huge bunch of sunset-coloured gladioli from the flower display outside the greengrocer's shop.

They were surprisingly heavy and I was struggling to keep the bunch upright and at the same time find my keys at the bottom of my briefcase, when I noticed a figure standing outside my front door, looking up and down the street.

'Can I help you?' I said.

The woman turned around. She was looking at a speaking bunch of gladioli. I peered through the stalks. She was in her early sixties, nicely dressed, if you liked a kind of conservative county style. She wore glasses.

'I doubt it,' she said in quite a hostile voice.

'Well, would you mind getting out of my way, then,' I said.

She moved somewhat reluctantly and started walking slowly up the road. At the time, I didn't give her another thought.

Chapter Fifteen

'So what was that all about, the other day?' I asked Jools in the steam room. 'You never told me that you knew the owner of this place.'

I got up painfully. The warmth of the steam had done very little to ease the almost total muscle seizure I had suffered since my work-out on Monday. It would be a long time before I ventured into the gym again. It took me a while to drag my clothes back on, and longer for Jools to complete her ablutions.

She was in an extremely chatty mood, pressing me on the latest developments with Dave.

Just when I had thought I would never hear from him again, he had rung, suggesting we meet on the night that happened also to be Dan's publication party. I wasn't altogether sure that I wanted him to come to that, but I found myself inviting him anyway. I couldn't quite work out what the status of my relationship with Dave was meant to be.

'He blows hot and cold. I mean, I don't know whether we're just becoming friends who occasionally have sex, or whether it's a relationship, or what,' I tried to explain. 'I don't know how I'm going to introduce him.'

It sounded like a dilemma from *Jackie* magazine. What are you meant to call your boyfriend when you're out of your teens? Call me suburban, if you like, but lover has adulterous connotations to my ears, and partner is too smugly PC; my guy is too fifties American and my man too sixties Liverpool. Friend is a bit coy, other half a bit presumptuous after one bonk.

'Well, does it matter?' asked Jools.

No, it didn't, I supposed, but it did seem odd to be able to be so utterly abandoned with someone at night and yet not have anything other than a perfectly ordinary conversation with him otherwise.

'Somehow, I just don't feel it's very deep,' I said to Jools, trying to explain.

'Sounds ideal,' said Jools. 'In my experience, so-called deep men are usually self-obsessed wankers who get so interested in talking about themselves, you're usually too bored or tired for sex afterwards.'

I burst out laughing, recognizing the type.

'Give yourself a break, for God's sake. You've got a gorgeous toy boy who's fantastically fuckable and wants reasonably regular sex. And you think that's a problem?'

'OK, OK!' I protested. 'Who was that mystery man in the green suit I saw you with the other day, by the way?'

'Oh, you mean Frank . . .'

'Yeah.'

'Well, Frank's a photographer I know, and I was setting it up for him to take some photos here. I mean, don't you think it would be a great place for a catalogue?'

'Great publicity for the place,' I said.

'Yeah,' said Jools. 'Harry took a bit of convincing. He thought we were talking about a girlie-calendar type thing – you know, topless girls bobbing up and down on the step machine, that kind of thing. These health-club owners are a bit sensitive about their reputations. Talking of sleaze, did you ever hear from that bloke with cowboy boots again?' asked Jools.

It took me a moment to think who she meant.

'You mean Nat? No. Mars is always doing that. He introduces me to a producer who seems really keen, we go out for a drink, he promises to come back to me with a proposition, and that's the last I hear of it. Although I never did think Nat was a very good bet . . .'

'You don't think your rendition of Roberta Flack had anything to do with it?'

'What do you mean?' I asked, mystified.

'Well, you sang us all "The First Time Ever I Saw Your Face" at the end of the evening, and it was just a tiny bit flat . . .'

'Christ, I didn't, did I? Roberta Flat,' I said, wincing with embarrassment. 'Well, no wonder, then. So when does the shoot begin?' I wanted to change the subject.

'The what? Oh, right. Soon. When Frank gets the lighting sorted,' said Jools.

'It's funny,' I said. 'He didn't look like a photographer. I thought they all had ponytails,' I mused.

'Appearances can be deceptive. Know what I mean?' said Jools, I thought unnecessarily defensively. I decided to drop the subject.

The party was already in full swing when I arrived. I had gone home to change after work, which had been a mistake, because there were major delays on the Northern Line, which made me rather more than fashionably late. In my haste to make up time, I had forgotten to bring my invitation with me. The girl on the door of the party room looked me up and down and asked me to sign the guest book. She then made a great show of reading my name aloud and checking it against her invitation list. I was beginning to feel less than welcome, when she said, disbelievingly, 'Oh, here you are, right at the top,' as if that were the place where the uncool people were listed. 'OK, then. Go in.'

I was just taking a glass of champagne from a waiter's tray when Donny spotted me across the room and came rushing over, nearly knocking the drink out of my hand.

'At last, a real person,' he said. 'I am bored to tears by these literary types.' I could see he had been drinking, and his camp voice was even louder than usual. Several people shifted away from us.

'And may I say that you're looking divine, if a teensy-weensy bit overdressed.'

'Sssh. It's bad enough having to brazen it out, without you shouting it all over the room,' I hissed.

As soon as I walked into the room, I had sensed that my Helen Storey black linen dress was overdoing it. It was clear that most of the people at the party had come straight from work and although the clothes were smart, they had a kind of sat-in-all-daytime look. Since I hadn't been to a party for ages, I had gone for something a bit glamorous. My black dress was plain enough, if very short, but the black quilted velvet mules with silver cherubs blowing silver trumpets at one another across my instep should really have stayed in their dark-green Miranda Moss box until Christmas. I had bought them in her January sale as a birthday present for myself, along with a matching quilted velvet evening bag with a silver cherub dangling from the drawstring, and this was the first vaguely suitable occasion there had been to wear them.

'Hallo, Sophie.'

I was surprised to see Stephanie, my friend who is addicted to alternative therapies, at a party in the Groucho Club.

'What are you doing here?' I asked, then, thinking

that sounded rude, added, 'I mean, I didn't know you knew Dan.'

We had all been at Cambridge together in the early eighties, but Donny and Dan were acting friends and Stephanie was a college friend. I usually tried keeping the various cliques I belonged to apart. I vividly remembered Donny saying once, 'Isn't it *awful* when you introduce one set of friends to another? Terrible if they don't get on. Somehow even *worse* if they do.' I knew exactly what he meant.

'I don't know him, exactly . . .' Stephanie was saying. 'I'm on my own now . . .'

I contorted my face into a look of sympathy, before realizing that she was talking about her business.

'. . . and I'm doing some personal PR as well as the corporate stuff.'

'Oh, great,' I said. 'Congratulations! What's your company called?'

'Well, I wanted to call it ESP, standing for Ethically Sound Publicity,' she replied, self-mockingly adding, 'and Green anything just doesn't sound attractive, so I'm just using my name. I do try to keep to PC accounts though.'

'How interesting,' I said. I had always found it odd that, given her leanings towards Buddhism and aromatherapy, Stephanie was an amazingly astute businesswoman. It was a tribute to her acumen that she had now engineered a way of combining her two strengths in a fashionable and growing market.

'Are you still promoting the holistic holidays?' I asked.

'Yeah. They've been so successful, they're opening another centre in the Caribbean next year. You must come. You look as if you need a holiday.'

'Thanks a lot.'

'No, I didn't mean . . . I mean, you look great, but have you attained inner peace yet?'

'Oh, don't start . . .' I said.

Stephanie is always on the look-out for a convert to a life-changing therapy. I was beginning to remember why it was that we hadn't seen each other for a while. I find large doses of Stephanie a bit wearing.

'Call me some time soon,' she said, moving on with the practised ease of a hostess. 'And do try the food. It's macrobiotic, but no one's guessed!'

I looked around the room for Donny, who had sidled off as soon as Stephanie started talking to me. He was standing by the door on his own and staring blearily into the crowd.

'I'm afraid I couldn't bring myself to rescue you, Sophie, dear,' he said. 'Who on earth is that woman? I mean, tofu and raw fish at a launch party, can you believe it?'

'Well, it's better than the normal canapés, isn't it?' I countered, picking a piece of sushi off a passing tray.

'Apparently so, my dear. Your friend also informed me that the seaweed wrapping was beneficial to the immune system . . . How very thoughtful . . . Of course, she needn't have bothered . . .'

I had a moment's panic. Donny was slurring his words, he was talking about immune systems, surely he wasn't about to announce that he was HIV-positive? I braced myself.

'She needn't have bothered. I'm such a queen that people are always thinking I'm at risk. Even you, dear Sophie, I see that worried look cross your brow – don't think I don't notice – but the awful fact is – ' he held on to the moment with theatrical timing – 'that I'm completely boring and monogamous. I've never loved anyone but Daniel. We're utterly middle-aged in our sex life. That most dreadful of words – companionable, really. What a dreadful word, Soph. But I wonder about Dan. He writes about promiscuity and death, and I do wonder, Sophie, I can tell you this, because you're a friend . . . I wonder, you know, whether he is being completely honest with the reader.'

'Or with you?' I ventured.

After nearly ten years' friendship, and three glasses of champagne, you can say things like that.

'Or with me.' Donny sighed, then the words seemed to register and he started. 'You're not trying to tell me something, are you?' he said, agitated.

'No. I'm not. As far as I know Dan feels just the same way about you. He simply wishes you wouldn't get so tetchy and critical about his work. He's a famous writer now, Donny, and you're going to have to learn to live with it.'

'You're quite right, of course.' Donny sighed again. His eyes drifted towards the door and then suddenly lit up. I automatically followed his gaze.

'Now there, my dear Sophie, is something that might tempt even me out of my middle-aged complacency . . .'

'You mean the beautiful boy who has just walked in?' I was preoccupied with wondering how Dave had managed to get past the frosty woman on the door. 'Well, dream on, Don, because he's with me.'

'But I saw him first . . .' exclaimed Donny.

'Wrong. I invited him.' I pushed my way through the crowd to greet Dave, who was looking somewhat bewildered.

'You've got some catching up to do,' I said, handing him a glass of champagne. 'How did you manage to negotiate your way in, by the way?' I whispered.

'I think she thought I was someone else,' he said. 'Long time, no see,' he added as he put his arms around me and kissed me properly.

I was kind of embarrassed and wriggled free, but when I saw the look of envy on the face of the girl at the door, I put my arm through Dave's and decided to show off a little. It was a long time since I had been out with anyone who was prepared to demonstrate their affection for me so publicly and I had forgotten how nice it felt.

I pulled him across the room to introduce him to Dan, who was talking to a very tall, slim man who had his back to us.

'Dan,' I interrupted, 'I want you to meet . . .'

I stopped mid-sentence. Dan's companion had turned around to face me. Although he had shaved his head and peroxided the remaining stubble, he was instantly recognizable as Gregory Murtagh, the unrequited love of my life.

'You've cut off your hair,' I blurted.

'Hi, Sophie,' he replied.

'Dan, this is Dave,' I said hastily, remembering my manners. 'Dave, Dan. Greg, Dave. Dave, Greg. Dan – oh, you two already met.' I was feeling extremely flustered.

'I've never met an author before,' said Dave, shaking Dan's hand.

'But why?' I said to Greg, pointing at his pale suede head, as soon as I felt the others were launched into conversation.

'I'm playing the lead in the film of Daniel's first novel,' said Greg. 'We're filming in the East End.'

I tried to convince myself that he looked less attractive with no hair, but if anything it made his eyes look bigger and the dark fringe of lashes longer. He hadn't lost the habit, remaining from the time when his long glossy black curls flopped over his face, of stroking his left hand across his cheek to push the hair behind one ear. But now there was no hair to push, the movement made him look oddly, endearingly vulnerable.

'Still in your bijou penthouse flat?' Greg asked.

'Yes,' I said. 'And you? Still in Dublin?'

'Most of the time. The film industry's really taking off over there.'

'So I hear,' I said. 'And Maeve?' I hated myself for it, but I couldn't stop asking about the girlfriend he had been on the point of ditching for me, before things went wrong between us.

'Yeah,' he answered enigmatically. 'And Dave?' he added, nodding in his direction.

I stifled a giggle at the rhyme our respective partners' names made.

'Yeah,' I said, trying to put as much mystery into my voice as he had into his.

Dave was animatedly describing the plot of *Misery* to Dan, who was doing a good job of pretending to look interested.

'And the weird thing is that there's someone in Sophie's life at the moment, she's no idea who, who keeps . . .'

'Actually, they've stopped. Must have been a case of mistaken identity,' I said, interrupting quickly. I elbowed Dave quite hard in his ribs.

As I hadn't received a single phone call, let alone a card, for over a week now, I was feeling rather embarrassed at having made such a fuss the last time I saw Dave.

'Dan, darling!!!' Dan's publisher, one of London's most flamboyant women, grabbed his arm and dragged him off to meet one of her other protégés. She failed to recognize me, even though I had done a week's temping for her earlier that year. I had read a number of news-paper articles about her editorial genius and her fervent feminist views, but neither of these qualities was blindingly obvious to her female employees. I pulled a face at her departing back, and tried to tune into the conversation going on beside me, without appearing to be overly interested.

'I've never met an actor before,' Dave was saying.

I noticed that no one had said, 'I've never met a nurse before,' when he told them what he did. They just affected a brief look of interest, then continued talking about themselves. Greg, however, with his natural gentle charm, asked, 'Now what made you decide to go into nursing?'

'Plenty of pretty girls,' said Dave and winked.

Greg chuckled.

I was horrified. It's bad enough having your present boyfriend talking to the old flame you've never quite got over, without them becoming lads together. I looked around the room for someone to talk to, but people were gradually slipping away. A couple of gossip columnists were getting steaming drunk in one corner.

Then I heard Greg say he was meeting his director for supper downstairs and would we like to join them.

'Food, yeah, great,' said Dave.

But I firmly declined, knowing that I had drunk far too much to be trusted to sit sandwiched between my past and present lovers without saying something I would regret in the morning.

'Really nice idea, but we're going on to dinner,' I said.

'Are we?' said Dave, as if it was the first time he had heard of it. Which it was.

It was later than I thought and the only restaurants

still open were Chinese. I think duck was a mistake at that time of night, but it could have been the four bottles of Tsingtao beer, on top of all that champagne, that made me spend most of the rest of the night hunched over my avocado-coloured toilet bowl.

Chapter Sixteen

I was feeling horribly fragile. Dave had insisted that I kept up my fluid intake during the night, and he brought me a cup of weak tea before he left in the morning, but I was still nauseous, and my brain seemed to be bouncing uncushioned against the inside of my skull.

'Perhaps I've got a virus?' I said weakly to Dave.

'You've got a hangover,' said Dave. 'It's probably done more harm to you than a virus, if that's any comfort.'

'No, I've had hangovers before. I'm sure this is something worse,' I protested.

'Drink lots of fluids and take it easy. You'll feel a lot better this evening. By the way, I'm going to the Isle of Wight for the weekend, to visit my aunt,' he added.

'Oh,' I said, feeling brushed off and sorry for myself.

'Wanna come?' he asked, and I suddenly felt a lot better.

I rang Dawn, the receptionist. Since I had spoken to her about my anonymous calls she had become quite chatty. If she was the person who had been calling me anonymously, she had decided to stop, and if she wasn't, the fact that I had confided in her must have made her more warmly disposed towards me. We smiled at each other every day now, and sometimes had a brief chat while I waited for the lift.

'I think I've got a virus,' I said.

'Heavy night, was it?' she joked, before connecting me to Martin.

'Martin, I'm really sick. I think I've got a virus,' I said, putting on a tiny, wavering voice.

'Good party?' Martin asked. I had forgotten that I'd told him about Dan's launch.

'All right, I've got a bloody awful hangover,' I said in my normal voice. 'Medically it's probably worse than a virus, if you must know.'

'OK, OK, Soph. I'll see you on Monday. Have a good weekend,' said Martin amiably.

That was easy enough. I snuggled back among the pillows, feeling thrilled and only slightly guilty about my truancy, and closed my eyes.

I had just fallen into a blissful doze when there was a knock at my door. I ignored it.

A few moments later there was another knock and Liz's voice said, 'Sophie? Are you there?'

Sighing, I wrapped myself in my sheet and went to the door.

'Hi. What's up?' I asked.

'Oh. You are there. It's just, you know, I couldn't help hearing you in the night . . . and then you didn't go out to work . . . and I just wanted to check to see if you were OK.'

'God, I feel even worse now that you've told me that,' I said. It was bad enough throwing up all night, without the knowledge that someone was hearing every retch. I vowed never to drink again. 'I think I've got a stomach virus.'

'Oh dear. There's a lot of it at work, too,' said Liz. 'Is there anything I can do?'

'No, thanks. That's really kind, but I'm just going to sleep it off, I think,' I said.

'I could easily take the day off,' said Liz. 'If you wanted.'

'No, really,' I said, wishing that I had just been honest about my hangover. It was too late to admit it now. I was grateful that Liz was expressing due concern about my state of health instead of sneering like the others had done, but I slightly wished that she would just mind her own business.

There's nothing I would hate more than the sort of neighbour who keeps popping round for a chat on the pretext of borrowing a cup of sugar. (Why, I wondered, was it always a *cup* of sugar? Most people didn't use sugar very much, and a spoonful would normally be enough to satisfy a sweet-toothed craving. Perhaps the cliché had its roots in the days when people actually made cakes. Whatever the facts, no neighbour would have much luck with me, since I didn't have any sugar in the house. Not even metaphorically.) I was giving myself a headache again.

'Look,' I said, firmly and wearily, 'I need to lie down.'

'I'll pop up and see how you are this evening,' said Liz.

Dave rang at lunchtime. I had slept deeply since Liz left and was feeling much better. He told me that he had arranged to borrow a car and wanted to leave after the rush hour. If I could get myself to Harrow-on-the-Hill tube, he would pick me up and we could drive straight off. It seemed more sensible than him driving all the way into town on a Friday night. I agreed.

I spent the afternoon trying to decide what to wear. It was a long time since I had been on a dirty weekend. The last one I could remember was with Jerry, my boss at the first bank. We had flown to Frankfurt, but the only glimpse I had caught of Germany was on the hair-raising taxi ride from the airport to the city centre. We stayed all day in our room and I hadn't even opened the specially purchased weekend bag containing my specially purchased dirty-weekend clothes, except to take the scarlet silk teddy Jerry had bought me at Heathrow out of the side pocket.

Jerry had dinner with the client, I had room service and watched a surprisingly unsexy soft-porn film on the hotel video. When I finally pulled out my discreet little black jersey (no need to iron) number, which had cost a month's salary (and those days I was earning a respectable salary), and slipped down to the bar for a drink, I had been taken for a prostitute three times before I reached the bottom of my Singapore gin sling.

This time I decided to travel light, shoving a couple of pairs of spare knickers into an overnight bag, along with my bikini and a change of T-shirt.

It was a very humid day and, since I didn't feel much like walking, I opted to take a cab to Finchley Road tube. As I waited for a free one at the bottom of Primrose Hill, I noticed a figure I recognized on the other side of the road. It was the elderly woman I had encountered the other day outside my building. She was hurrying along, too preoccupied to notice me, looking at her watch, as if she were late for some appointment. When she reached the delicatessen on the opposite side of the street from my flat, she stopped. I thought she had gone into the shop, but as my taxi drove past, I saw that she was standing in the doorway, staring fixedly up at my window.

Dave's aunt, Norma, was the manageress of a holiday

camp. She was a lovely, friendly London woman, with a big blonde wig, who chain-smoked and told risqué jokes all the time. She and her husband had run a large pub in Hounslow, but he had died young, and she had used the insurance money to buy the run-down camp that had been deserted by its regular customers as they discovered they could get sunshine in Spain for the price of rain in England. She had always wanted to live by the sea, she said, and she had seen possibilities for the camp that everyone else had missed. She catered solely for groups of disabled people.

'It's ideal, you see,' she said, showing us to one of the bungalows that fanned out from the main building. 'It's all on one level and there's no steps.'

Dave came down one weekend every month, when her regular nurse and helper had his weekend off.

'Don't worry, love,' Norma said to me and winked. 'I won't work him too hard. I just need a bit of help getting them all into dinner, and then, if you want to join in, we're having a Country and Western evening.'

I'd never had much experience of disabled people before, and I was nervous at first, but watching Dave and the way he treated everyone completely normally, judging exactly when a helping hand was needed without ever compromising anyone's dignity, was an education to me. I soon relaxed and we had a riotous evening, ending with me and Norma singing 'Islands in the Stream', with me as a slightly squeaky Kenny Rogers, Norma a natural Dolly Parton.

On Saturday Dave drove me round the island. The weather had been so hot recently, there was a heat haze that made it impossible to see the mainland. I felt as if we were cocooned in a time warp. The little seaside towns seemed untouched since the sixties. Tea-shops still offered old-fashioned items like cinnamon toast and the ice-cream floats that I remembered as treats from holidays with Mum.

There was a barn dance that evening. I could never have imagined doing a do-si-do with a partner in a wheelchair until I found myself doing it.

Later, Dave and I returned to our bungalow, glowing from a day's sea air and the evening's dancing, and fell into bed with a hunger for each other that we had not felt before.

That night I was so carried away by glorious sensation that I found myself wanting to say 'I love you', because 'that feels so good' didn't seem to capture adequately just how wonderful it did feel. I managed to stop myself. My treacherous body has made me say those three fateful words to several men during sex, and it always leads to disaster. However much you babble afterwards about the paucity of the language of sex, insisting that you didn't mean it *like that*, they never believe you.

It was difficult to gauge how Dave was feeling. He appeared to possess an exceptionally even temperament and I had yet to see him angry, or sad, or moody, or even excited. For someone as up and down as me, this could be difficult to deal with, and once or twice I had to stop myself provoking a reaction from him.

On the way back to London, neither of us said much. It was almost as if we didn't want to spoil a perfect weekend. Dave dropped me off at home. He was going straight into work. We kissed briefly in the car and I waved after him as he pulled away up the hill.

The flashes on my answerphone indicated that there

were two messages. When I played them back, they were both hang-ups, but there was a disturbing quality to the silences, as if the caller were waiting and listening before putting down the phone. The calls could have come from anyone – friend or wrong number – but I was absolutely certain that I knew who it was. My mystery caller had resurfaced, and, more worryingly, she now knew where I lived.

I felt slightly panicky. It seemed ridiculous to be frightened by thirty seconds of silence on an answerphone, but I was. Mum and Reg weren't due back for another week, Dave was on his way to work. It was nearly midnight. It didn't seem worth getting Donny and Dan out of bed and explaining everything to them, but I wanted to talk to someone. I decided to brave Martin's derision and ring him. I was dialling his number, when there was a knock on my door. I froze.

'Sophie? Is that you?' said Liz's voice.

I opened the door with a huge sigh of relief.

'Hi,' I said.

'Nice weekend?' she asked. She was dressed for bed, wearing a sensible but unattractive dressing gown. It made her look older.

'Very, thanks. Fancy a coffee or something?' A glance at my watch told me that it was only ten-thirty.

'No, thanks,' she said, in quite a clipped way.

'Hot chocolate then – I've got all flavours.' I had been tempted by a trial pack of ten flavoured diet drinks on my recent trawl round Sainsbury's.

'No,' she said, adding, 'You might have told me.'

'What?' I asked bemused.

'You might have told me you were going away. The last time I saw you, you were ill. I said I'd come up on

Friday evening. I brought you some supper from the Food Hall. Just something light, you know, for your stomach. Then there's no reply from you . . . I was quite worried.'

'Oh, I'm sorry,' I said. 'Look, that was really kind of you, I didn't think . . . sorry.'

'It was lucky I saw the landlord, and he said he'd seen you skipping off with an overnight bag. I . . . I just didn't know what to do when there was no reply.' She looked close to tears.

'Hey, I'm really sorry,' I said. 'That was thoughtless of me. I'm so used to living on my own, I'm just not used to anyone noticing my comings and goings,' I added, with what I thought was the appropriate balance of gratitude and mind-your-own-business in my tone. It was sweet of Liz to be so concerned, but I was beginning to feel slightly smothered.

She seemed to brighten.

'As long as you're OK,' she said.

'I'm fine,' I said. I paused for a second, debating inwardly whether to tell her about the messages on my answerphone. No, I decided. I would never hear the last of it. And anyway, it was probably just Mum trying to get through from Italy, I told myself.

'Are you sure you won't come in?' I asked slightly insincerely.

'No. I'd better get some sleep,' she said.

Chapter Seventeen

'D'you fancy a Thai lunch, Miss Fitt?'

'Ooh, Mr Young, that sounds exotic,' I said, putting on a silly Kenneth Williams-type voice.

Martin and I seemed to be unconsciously developing a way of coping with our working relationship by improvising a kind of *Carry On up the For. Ex.* comedy routine whenever we spoke to each other at the bank.

'I'd like a spring roll, Miss Fitt,' Martin responded with a wink.

'Oh, honestly, Martin,' I said, cringing at his joke, but pleased with the invitation.

Before I started working for him, Martin and I used to meet for lunch or a drink at least once a week. These days, although I saw him every day, it was usually for about five minutes each day, and that was normally to take dictation.

We ordered the mixed starters, which arrived decorated with roses carved from carrots, with several doll's-house dishes of different sauces. I tasted a fish cake, delicately spiced with coriander seed, and decided immediately to award the restaurant four stars in my restaurant file.

'How did you find this place?' I asked Martin.

'I came here with my vice-president,' he replied. 'Oh, sorry!' A small globule of peanut sauce shot out of his mouth and landed in my beer. 'Another Singha beer, please.' He smiled at the passing waitress.

'Great food,' I said, dipping a tiny rolled pancake that contained a sprig of fresh coriander and a tiger prawn into a little saucer of sweet chilli sauce.

'Thank you very much,' said Martin and smiled again, his most winning smile, at the waitress who had just replaced my beer.

'Oh, you haven't come here to ogle the waitresses, have you? For God's sake, Martin,' I said.

'Not at all,' said Martin.

'Honestly, you're such a cliché when it comes to women,' I continued, warming to my theme. 'If it's not an air-hostess, it's an oriental waitress.'

I was referring to an ex of Martin's called Darryl. She used to live upstairs from Martin. Unwisely, since they had nothing at all in common, they started a relationship. It continued for a year or so, with Martin growing more and more miserable, but feeling too guilty to get out of it, when suddenly she left, leaving Martin a note saying that she had gone to live with a recently divorced pilot, with whom, it transpired, she had been having an affair all the time. Martin hadn't known whether to feel relieved or offended.

'I suppose your idea of heaven is a long-haul flight on Singapore Airlines,' I finished.

'Don't be ridiculous, I was just being polite. Anyway, I never pass comment on your boyfriends.'

'Ha!' I said triumphantly. 'So you *are* interested in the waitress . . . Anyway, that's not true. You were horrible about Jerry . . .'

'So were you.'

'And you thought that Greg was a narcissistic Irish poofter. I quote.'

'That was only to cheer you up when he chucked you.'

'Ouch!' I said, wanting to change the subject before he started giving me his impressions of Dave.

We both fell silent for a few moments while the starters were cleared away and steaming bowls of tom yum soup, fragrant with lemon grass, were put before us.

'Seriously, Soph, there is something I wanted to talk to you about,' said Martin, blowing on his soup.

'Yeah?' I didn't like his tone of voice.

'The thing is, there has been a complaint about you,' he said, shifting in his chair and avoiding eye contact.

'What? From whom? Not the receptionist, surely? I've been in virtually on time . . .'

'No,' Martin interrupted. 'Not from Dawn, nor Marie, nor Pat, actually . . . Well, I don't know how to put this, but from higher up. You see, they tape all the calls and they do random checks . . .'

'They what?' I spluttered. 'Are you telling me that someone up there is listening in to all the calls made from the bank?'

'Well, not all the time, obviously. Not usually unless there's a dispute – you know, a question about any of the deals . . . millions of dollars go through that dealing room some days.'

I had always thought it was a little strange that the only evidence of foreign exchange deals were the scribbled scraps of paper which the dealers churned out by the hundred every day and which were logged by two typists who worked under Pat's jurisdiction. But I had no idea that all the lines were bugged.

'They've been doing random checks, recently . . . I think it's kind of unlucky, but they've caught you twice having conversations of over an hour with a guy who obviously has nothing to do with work . . . and once he was in New York.'

'Dan?'

'I suppose so. I mean, I'm sorry to have brought it up, but, you know, I was brought in as Mr Clean, and it looks a bit bad.'

'God, I'm sorry, Martin,' I said. 'I had no idea, really. It won't happen again. You might have told me, though.'

'I thought you knew. Most banks have installed that system nowadays.'

'Well, whoever it was must have been surprised. As I recall, our conversations ranged from death to literature to the death of literature, but we hardly touched on finance . . .'

Martin tried to look very stern, but then we both spontaneously started giggling.

'Why were you brought in as Mr Clean, by the way?' I asked, adding, 'and don't tell me it's confidential . . . In the days before I worked for you, you never had a problem telling me anything.'

'I know. I know.' He leant forward conspiratorially. 'Well, if you promise not to tell anyone . . .'

'Oh, yeah, Martin, I'll go straight back to the office and ring up everyone I know, especially all my friends in New York.'

'Well, OK. The bank fired my predecessor because he had a bit of a problem with Charlie.'

'Charlie who?' I dabbed my eyes with a napkin. The soup had a dangerous quantity of little white chilli seeds in it. The heat was making my eyes run.

'Charlie, Soph, you know, begins with c, it's a euphemism for . . .'

'Oh, *coke*!' I said, finally cottoning on.

'Sssh. Well, he was spending so much time in the toilets that his performance was suffering, and so were a number of the dealers. There was a bit of a purge . . .'

'Oh, my God. Was there a raid, with police and everything?' I inquired.

'No. Not as far as I know. No hard evidence, you see. They might have had a few incriminating calls on tape, but nothing that would stand up in court.'

'And it's bad publicity,' I added. There had to be a more venal reason where the bank was concerned.

'Right.' Martin looked a bit ashamed. 'Yeah, confidence is pretty low at the moment. They didn't want a whole load of drugs prosecutions too, with headlines about City dealers and all the puns to go along with it.'

'So they just made a bunch of guys redundant and nobody knew why?' I asked, incredulous.

'Yeah. Don't look at me like that, Soph. It wasn't my decision, you know. It was before I joined, and, no, I didn't know about it before I joined either, before you start jumping to conclusions.'

I believed him.

'So that's why all the guys are afraid of you, and morale's so low?' I said.

In a way it was a relief to know the truth. I thought Martin looked relieved, too, although I could understand why he hadn't wanted to tell me. His natural sense of fair play would have prevented him from telling me something which nobody else in the room officially knew.

'Yeah.'

'And I mistook it for your natural authority,' I said, trying to lighten up the atmosphere, and failing.

'What with that, and Denise's death ... she was popular, I gather, and it's difficult to make sense of something like that,' said Martin despondently.

I looked at our main courses. We hadn't made much impression on them.

'I got another couple of those calls,' I said. The atmosphere was becoming pervasively gloomy.

'Oh, no. I thought you said they'd stopped. This morning?'

'No. At home at the weekend. They were only silences, but it was the same person.'

'Silences?' repeated Martin.

'Yeah, on my answerphone. There were two messages, but no one spoke,' I said.

'So how could you possibly . . .'

'. . . know who it was?' I finished his sentence for him. 'I just did. Don't you believe me?'

I was glad that I had eventually decided not to ring Martin the night before. One of the benefits of having an inadequately soundproofed house and a nosy neighbour, I had decided, was that I couldn't come to much harm without someone being aware of it.

'Course I believe that you believe it,' Martin was saying, 'but that doesn't necessarily mean it's true . . .'

'Oh, hell,' I said. 'Why are you always so bloody unimaginative? Honestly, Martin, if I weren't so broke, I'd quit right now. It's bad enough sitting next to Porsche-driving yuppies who are probably putting more than my weekly salary up their noses, without working for a boring boss who's doing a good impression of being middle-aged before his thirtieth birthday.'

'Sorry, Soph,' said Martin and waved his Amex card at the waitress.

That afternoon I rang Mars. I didn't hold out much hope of him getting me work, but he was bound to invite me out and tell me how talented I was, and I needed a bit of a confidence boost.

'Sophia, Sophia,' he exclaimed, making my name rhyme with admire, which I hate. 'I was just about to ring you.'

'Really, Mars?' I said sceptically.

'Upon my soul.'

'I didn't know you had one,' I said.

'Now, now,' he said. 'Where are you staying in Edinburgh? We must meet up.'

I had put Edinburgh entirely out of my mind. My spirits sank.

'Not going,' I said glumly. 'Can't afford to.'

'We must do something about this appalling money situation of yours. Are you sure you won't reconsider Nat's proposal?'

'Proposal?' I echoed, trying not to sound too inquisitive. Something must have been said on the night of my Roberta Flack rendition. I must have blotted it out, along with all the other bits of the evening my subconscious preferred not to remember.

'This game-show thing. I know it's not really what you're looking for, but it could be fun. And he does pay. Several of my clients have worked for him, and, you know, they say it's falling-off-a-log time.'

'How much?' I said.

'Five hundred a piece. For a day's work. Listen, pop along to his studio tomorrow for a screen test.' He said that he would ring Nat and fix an audition for lunchtime. He gave me an address in the East End.

'And let's get together after Edinburgh. Kick around a few ideas. Mwaa. Mwaa,' he said and rang off.

The prospect of another month's frugality was a gloomy one. I looked in my fridge that evening and saw that all the salad vegetables had passed their eat-by date some

time ago. They smelt rather unpleasant. I closed the
fridge door. Five hundred pounds would make a lot of
difference to my life right now. I stared out of my
window and down at the delicatessen across the road,
trying to convince myself that I didn't want one of their
freshly made ciabatta rolls for supper. The elderly woman
stared back at me from the doorway.

Chapter Eighteen

From the outside, Nat's production office looked like a derelict warehouse. I rang the bell, which had a Post-it note saying Nat. Ent. stuck on to it. There was no reply, so I rang again, pushing harder.

'Zoe!' Nat opened the door. '*Entrez!* Come in! How *are* you?' He didn't wait for a greeting in return. 'I'm told that Zoe means life. Am I right?'

'Yes, you are,' I said. 'But my name's Sophie, which means wisdom. Sorry to be pedantic.'

'Whatever turns you on . . .' he replied, smiling. There was something different about his face. He had grown a droopy moustache that made him look sleazier than ever.

I should have just turned around and left that moment.

Instead, I stepped over the threshold. The floor was stone and in need of a good sweeping. There were bits of packaging lying around and the corridor into the main part of the building was lined with boxes on each side, making it so narrow we had to move in single file. The boxes were plain brown, but some had yellow labels facing out. I managed to read the words GENUINE LATEX upside-down, and then noticed that someone had scrawled with a substantial felt-tip pen on some of the rows the words TIQUE and on others TAKE and DRESS.

Nat made banal conversation until we arrived in the main body of the building, or space, as he called it.

There were two girls with blood-red lipsticked mouths, wearing black micro-skirts and Dr Martens, sitting on more boxes which said GUIDED on the side. One of them had a nose ring.

'Make yourself at home! Draw up a *pew*, as you English say!'

I hadn't heard anyone say that for years. I wondered where Nat was 'coming from'.

'The others aren't quite so punctual, little Miss Fitt.'

At least he had remembered my second name. I smiled patiently.

'Excuse me,' he said. 'I hear the *bell*!'

He did a dreadful impersonation of Charles Laughton which was obviously designed to attract laughter, but both the other girls and I sat there glumly as he left the room.

I coughed and ventured a smile at each of them.

'I'm wardrobe,' said the one with the nose ring, in a flat south London voice.

'Oh, yeah? So I suppose you're Lion and I'm Witch,' I said brightly. There wasn't even a glimmer of a smile in response.

'I bet you get that all the time?' I added, with less confidence.

'Nah, I'm make-up,' said the other.

'I'm Sophie.' I couldn't think what else to say.

'Thought he said you was called Zoe.'

'He did. But he was wrong. My name is Sophie.'

'Oh, right.' They exchanged glances as if they weren't sure who to believe.

'D'you wanna see your costumes, then?' asked Wardrobe, wearily heaving herself from her pile of boxes. 'Over here.'

In the dim recesses of the warehouse where there was

149

no natural light she showed me a rail on wheels with a few tired-looking sequined outfits hanging from it.

'Actually, I normally do my own clothes,' I said. I had a carrier bag with my props and a change of T-shirt in it. I invariably wear slim black trousers on stage with either a white T-shirt or a black T-shirt. If it's a particularly cold venue, I wear a black tuxedo on top. It's far too big for me, but it looks OK. I have a few pearls, hats, spectacles and scarves as decoration.

'This is for the first bit.' Wardrobe was holding up what looked like a turquoise bathing costume with a kind of chiffon mermaid's tail at the back. It was made of shiny Lycra and the sequins were purple.

'The colour suits you,' she said, holding the hanger near enough my face for me to catch a whiff of the previous wearer's sweat. 'Nat didn't say you was so small. I've got some safety pins with me, but I'll have to see if I can get hold of a smaller one for Friday.' She looked at me accusingly, as if my size was going to involve her in unpaid overtime.

I looked closely at her face to see if she was joking. There wasn't a glimmer of a smile.

'I can't wear that,' I said.

'Looks lovely on,' she said. 'Better on than off, if you get my drift. This –' she held up a thing (there wasn't enough of it to be called a garment) which had two silver triangles as a top and strings of rhinestones attaching that to an even smaller triangle with a thong – 'is for the second bit. It's OK,' she said, seeing the expression of horror that was crossing my face. 'Trash'll give you an all-over tan. Doesn't look fake under the studio lights.'

'Trash?'

'Short for Tracy. Make-up.' She pointed at her friend.

'I think there has been a mistake,' I said.

Wardrobe looked offended and slouched off back to her box, where she whispered something to Trash and they both giggled.

The noise coming down the corridor indicated that Nat was returning with a bunch of people. They spilled into the room. There were four square-jawed men, all wearing white T-shirts and worn blue jeans, who looked as if they had walked out of an advertisement for a not particularly sophisticated deodorizing body spray (it turned out that they had in fact just been filming a non-alcoholic cider commercial), and three giggly teenage girls who all had the same short haircut but in different shades: blonde, copper and brunette. When they managed to stop tittering for more than a second, their faces took on a composure that was quite alarmingly mature and beautiful. I recognized this characteristic from Jools. They were obviously models.

They were followed by an older guy with a ponytail who was dressed in black and carried a couple of cameras with long lenses over his shoulder.

'Guys. Dolls. Introductions!' said Nat. 'This is Miss Fitt, your compere, and these, babe, are the contestants. My friend Cash will be taking some photos. OK?' He handed everyone except the photographer copies of a script. The contestants opened theirs obediently and started reading. I noticed that a couple of the men moved their lips as they followed the lines with one finger.

I flipped through the first few pages and then gestured to Nat that I wanted a word.

'Problems, Babe?'

'Could I talk to you privately a moment?' I asked.

There was an outbreak of giggling from the girls, as if I had said something risqué. Nat raised his eyebrows, playing to his audience.

151

'Sure, babe.'

I felt like saying that Zoe was better than babe, but saved it.

'Can you just run through the *concept* again,' I said, trying to find words he could connect with. 'Because the first *vibes* I'm getting are kind of . . . you know . . . bad.'

'Hey! Relax, babe.'

'I'm perfectly relaxed,' I said, trying to keep my temper.

'It's simple, babe,' he said, putting an unwelcome arm around me. 'You just ask the girls a question and if they're right they win a prize, if they're wrong they have to do a forfeit. The exciting thing about this show is that the guys 'n' dolls design the forfeit and like, it's kind of like the participants kind of determine where the show is going.'

'But the forfeits, as far as I can see, are in the script.'

'Yeah, as far as we're concerned they are . . . how else are you gonna shoot a show in a day? Get real, babe. But the viewer doesn't know that . . .'

'My other concern is that the forfeits involve taking off clothes, and that's only the beginning,' I said as calmly as I could. In a quick glance at the back of the script I had seen what I thought was a stage direction for fellatio.

'Not you, honey, no nudity for you. That sort things out for you, babe?'

'I just can't see why you want me for this role. All I do is ask revoltingly sexist questions,' I pressed on, even though he was getting a bit fidgety, anxious to move on.

'Jokes, ad lib, make the script *yours*, babe. Feel free.'

'But the costume. I can't possibly . . .'

Nat walked away.

I leafed through the script again, trying to visualize

what it would look like on the screen. I didn't want to prejudge, because I had no experience of reading television scripts, but it seemed to me that this was more pornography than game show. I tried to recall other light-entertainment shows I had seen recently. Certainly they were full of *double entendres*, and contestants might be made to make the odd suggestive remark, but nothing went this far.

'Let's get this show on the road.'

All the participants stood up and divided themselves into two groups of the same sex.

'Hey, where's girl four?' said Nat, as if it had only just occurred to him that the numbers were uneven.

God, I thought, I'm auditioning for someone who can't even count up to eight.

Girl four was apparently delayed at a photographic shoot for a book cover. Nat decided to go ahead without her.

'Babe, I'm camera one,' he instructed me. 'Look straight at me and introduce the first three and leave four out.'

I started reading half-heartedly from the script, looking up from time to time to see Nat making vertical circles in the air beside his right ear, like a maniac charade player pretending to be a film camera. The photographer danced around, clicking from the strangest angles.

'Our first doll is called Susie. She's a waitress. She'll offer you a service at any time of day!' I read flatly. 'Our second doll is Annie, she's a shop assistant, but what's her price? . . . Look, I just don't think I can read this stuff.'

'Well, make up something else then,' said Nat quite sharply. 'I thought you were into improvisation . . . Jesus! Just smile a lot, and wink at the camera, if you can manage that without a tantrum.'

153

I was so shocked by his tone, I did as he said.

'Here's Susie!' I said. 'She's an astronomer. What a star!' Grin, grin.

'Great!' said Nat, surprising me.

'And next is Annie . . .' The brunette stepped forward and smiled vacantly. 'She's a consultant haematologist. And finally Daisy . . . who is, erm, a professor of poetry with a particular interest in the iconography of Homer.' Wink.

'Super!' said Nat. 'Bit long, that last one, leave the homo stuff out . . . this show is strictly het . . . but great.'

I couldn't believe my ears. I was beginning to see what Mars had meant by alternative. This was positively anarchic.

'Now the guys,' said Nat.

'Here's Johnny! Let me see . . . erm . . . he's an astronaut and he's walking on air . . . and next is Andy, who's a professor of intellectual property law . . .'

'Too long,' said Nat. 'Try to keep all the intros the same length, but you're getting the hang of it. Just practise a bit, yeah? Happy?'

Everyone said yes.

'OK, then, take ten,' he said. 'There's a sandwich bar round the corner.' He and the photographer both rushed off to the loo. Wardrobe and Tracy, who had been watching the proceedings sullenly, left together, as did the bunch of beautiful people.

I sat down on a box and looked at my watch. Martin had said I could be as long as I wanted, but I didn't want to be away from the office for too long, especially since the complaints.

Nat came back into the room, looking a lot brighter.

'What station is this going to be on?' I asked. 'Even late at night, I just can't see it on the BBC, or even Carlton.'

'Hey, babe, it's like, it's kinda more of an international . . .'

'Satellite?' I interrupted.

'Well, maybe. At the moment we're talking more international video . . .'

'Video?' I was beginning to smell a rat.

'Well, it could always get bought for cable, of course. But first off . . .'

'Nat, cut the bullshit. When you say international, what exactly do you mean?' I asked.

'First orders are from Japan, honey, but normally we get most of the airport hotels. International ones, natch.'

'So that's why you don't mind what I say? It's all going to be dubbed over?' The penny was finally dropping.

'Well, in a manner of speaking . . .'

'In a manner of speaking, I'm not speaking. In fact, in a manner of speaking, I'm just a dumb blonde introducing a sex game . . . Am I right?' I was boiling inside, but my voice was ice cold.

'Err . . .' It was the first time I had ever seen Nat lost for words. It was the first time, I suddenly realized, I had seen him sober.

'I have just one question. Why me?' I inquired. 'If I have any talent at all, it's hardly as a porn star, surely. I haven't even got tits to speak of . . .'

'I know, honey,' said Nat, as if glad to have found something to agree about, 'but, trust me, I know the market. Japanese businessmen love blonde Western women, but they can be just too tall and kind of threatening. But you, babe, are physically perfect for them . . . And your name, Miss Fitt, it kind of goes in with my . . .'

'Well, if I ever get desperate I'll know where to go to

earn a buck,' I said, unable to bear any more of this. 'Downtown Tokyo. But in the meantime, Nat, you can take your video and stuff it up your . . .'

'Something wrong, babe?'

I thought of lots of brilliant and witty goodbyes to say to Nat, but only afterwards. At the time I simply shouted, 'Just fuck off, you filthy old git.' And, picking up my carrier bag of props and rushing out, I had to push past the returning beautiful people, not wanting them to see the tears in my eyes.

I bumped into Jools outside the bank. She had just done a work-out and was looking for a lunch companion.

'Not today,' I said.

'Go on. I've found this great place that does Tuscan food,' she said.

Martin had said I could have as much time as I wanted. What the hell, I thought.

'Can you remember life before grilled vegetables?' I asked as we sat down. 'I mean, why was it that millions of years after discovering fire, man only decided to put red peppers under flames *circa* 1989?'

'It's Italian, isn't it?' Jools offered, as if in explanation.

'And if you can't grill the veg, then for God's sake dry them, preferably in the sun. There you have porcini, for example,' I said, as Jools plonked down a large hand-painted ceramic bowl of steaming risotto, 'and I'd bet my life there are a number of sun-dried tomatoes lurking in that salad. The other day I even saw sun-dried auber-gines in Camisa's on Old Compton Street. I mean, the whole point of aubergine is that it is succulent and juicy and soaks up pints of olive oil. But don't start me on olive oil. When I was a child it only meant one thing – a pained expression and a lot of boasting about upset tummies from people rich enough to have been on holiday to Spain. Now, even the Spar on the corner has several varieties, and have you noticed that you don't pour it any more? The word is drizzle. It never pours but it drizzles. And . . .'

'Are you on something?' asked Jools, amazed at my ranting.

'No.'

'You just practising for the show, then?'

'No. Sorry. Just getting rid of some frustration. No, after today, I think my career in show business is definitely over.' I launched into a description of the so-called screen test.

With half an hour's hindsight, it already seemed quite amusing. Jools was shaking with laughter by the time I finished.

'I thought that Nat was a bit funny,' she said.

'Funny ha ha or funny peculiar?' I said.

A brief memory of my English teacher, a strict middle-aged woman who was rigorous about vocabulary, flitted through my mind. I used to do an impersonation of her in the copse at the bottom of the school playing-field, where we went to practise smoking, and where I would entertain my classmates by imitating the teaching staff.

Jools and I collapsed in giggles again.

'Seriously, though,' she said, 'you're lucky to have got out when you did. There's a lot of girls get persuaded to do a bit of "modelling" for money, and the photographer chats them up, and before they know it they're appearing from all angles on the top shelf of your local newsagent's. Or worse. Then they kind of lose their self-respect . . . it's a slippery slope . . .' She rattled on knowledgeably. I wondered how she knew so much about it. Perhaps there was more to her 'modelling' career than she was letting on.

'Well, I don't think there was much danger of that as far as I was concerned,' I interrupted her. 'Nat made it quite clear that my statistics were only suitable for export . . . I have to tell you,' I said, 'this is a real low point in my life. My career on the stage ends with me narrowly missing a leading role in a porn video, I'm being bugged at work, and there's a cranky old woman who keeps watching my flat. I think she must be the person who kept calling me. She just stands there and stares.'

'Hang on, you've lost me. Can I have that again, slowly?' said Jools.

I began to tell her what Martin had told me the day before at lunch.

'So you mean they record *all* the calls that come in and out of the bank?' asked Jools.

'Yeah. It's very Big Brotherish, isn't it?' I said. I almost started telling her about the drugs scandal, but remembered, just in time, my promise to Martin.

'Then there's this old woman. First of all I see her acting suspiciously outside my door and then she's staring at me from over the road,' I said, hurrying on to cover my tracks.

'Did you speak to her?' Jools asked.

'I did the first time. Just briefly . . . Well, I suppose it *could* have been the same voice as the one on the telephone.'

I wasn't sure. I'd wanted to check, so when I'd seen her standing outside the delicatessen again the night before I'd decided to try to engage her in conversation, but I'd met Liz coming in from work in the hall down-stairs and we'd chatted for a couple of minutes. By the time I opened the front door, the old woman was no-where to be seen.

'You see,' I continued, 'it's a while since I've had a call where she has actually spoken.'

'Is this old woman a derelict, homeless, that sort of thing?' asked Jools.

The thought hadn't occurred to me. I had been so busy thinking about myself, I hadn't really given her circumstances a thought. I was becoming a typical Londoner.

'I shouldn't think so,' I said, conjuring her up in my imagination. She looked clean and quite smartly dressed. I particularly remembered the tap-tap-tap on the pave-ment of her patent-leather Mrs Thatcher-style court shoes as she had hurried along the Friday before.

'Perhaps she's one of those weirdos they've let out of long-stay mental homes to be cared for in the commun-ity,' Jools offered.

'Oh, great!' I said. 'Denise was killed by one of those guys. That makes me feel a whole lot better.' I laughed, but then I started thinking out loud.

Why had Denise been doing a self-defence course? Perhaps she had been terrorized by anonymous phone calls and birthday cards too. Perhaps her death on the tube was not the random mugging that everyone seemed to assume it was. Perhaps she had known her assailant. Or had heard them on the phone . . .

'I love a good mystery,' Jools replied. 'I watch them all on the telly . . .' She didn't seem to be taking me seriously.

'So you don't think it could be linked to Denise?' I asked her, point blank.

'It would be a bit far-fetched, wouldn't it? Especially since they caught the bloke that did it,' said Jools.

I wondered how she knew this, but then remembered that Pat had told me the case had been in the papers. I chewed my focaccia and tapenade thoughtfully.

'How's Dave, anyway?' Jools asked.

I hadn't seen her since Dave and I had been to the Isle of Wight, so I gave her a detailed description.

'Hang on, this is the Isle of Wight, Sophie. You're making it sound like Corfu or something,' said Jools, adding, 'It must be love.'

'Well, I'm not sure about that, but it's the nearest I've been this year. We got on brilliantly, I really liked his aunt, I think his aunt liked me. Needless to say, he hasn't called since, and I still don't know where I stand . . .'

'Resist the temptation to ask,' said Jools wisely.

'Yeah. I'm not that desperate yet. I know what he'd say, anyway. He'd say that he wanted more space. Why do men always say that when they mean they want to end the relationship? I mean, when Jerry said it to me, it turned out that he meant 3,000 miles' more bloody space. An entire ocean's worth, in fact.'

Chapter Nineteen

Liz knocked on my door on Saturday afternoon and asked me whether I fancied an outing to the zoo. I had been trying to get up the enthusiasm for a run in the park. My telephone was resolutely refusing to ring and I was furious with myself for not having made any plans for the weekend, expecting Dave to call, so I was happy to have an excuse to go out. It was a lovely soft summer's day, which made a change from the muggy weather we had been having.

I had only bumped into Liz once briefly during the week, so my fears about her turning into an interfering neighbour had somewhat abated. She was pleasant, undemanding company, which was just what I needed at that moment, and she had a genuine enthusiasm for moments like the penguins' feeding time, which managed to charm me out of my self-pitying grumpiness. I watched her cuddling a lamb in the farm bit of the zoo that was meant for children. There was an absence of cynicism in her personality that made me curious to know more about her background.

She became shyly reticent when speaking about her family, but gradually a picture began to emerge. She was an only child of rather old parents. They had lived in a grocer's shop called Family Value Stores that her father owned in a small market town in East Anglia. He had apparently been a pillar of the local community and chairman of the Conservative Club. They had been very happy there, she said.

'So why did you all move to London?' I asked.

We were sitting having a cup of tea in a café, hoping to catch a glimpse of the elephants, who for some reason seemed unwilling to leave their house and display their bulk to the general public. Occasionally one would poke his trunk out of the door and sniff the summer air, then reverse back into the Elephant House.

Liz looked up.

'Oh, it all got a bit much for him, running the shop and everything. He applied for a job as a departmental manager in the Food Hall – you know, a steady job, with a pension and all that. We moved down to London. To Hackney. Mum still lives there.'

'How long ago?' I asked.

'We came to London when I was twenty. So I've lived here more than half my life.'

'You're over forty?' I spluttered, having just taken a mouthful of tea. 'But you look much younger.'

'Do I?' she said.

'I thought you were about my age,' I said, exaggerating slightly downwards.

'Oh, no,' said Liz, obviously surprised. 'I'm old enough to be your mother.'

'Not unless you started very young!' I laughed.

She blushed. I noticed that whenever the subject of sex came up, however indirectly, she became embarrassed. I had to keep reminding myself that Liz was very different from Jools.

'What about your family?' she asked.

'My mum's away at the moment, on honeymoon! Coming back next week, actually. She just got married again,' I said.

Apart from a postcard from Pompeii, I hadn't heard from Mum since the wedding. I could have done with some of her calming good sense over the past month. It was great to think she would be home in a few days' time.

'So you come from a broken home?' said Liz.

'Well, I suppose so,' I said. 'That makes it sound rather dysfunctional, though. Actually, I had a lovely childhood and I adore my stepfather.'

'You sound as if you were very happy,' said Liz wistfully.

'Yes. I was,' I said, feeling almost guilty that she looked so sad. Perhaps there were things in her childhood that she wasn't prepared to tell.

We gave up on the elephants and walked towards the exit.

'What's your favourite animal?' asked Liz, making an effort to brighten up.

'Oh, I don't know,' I said. 'I like the big cats. Lions, probably.'

'Leo the lion,' she replied. 'Do you believe in astrology?'

'No,' I replied. 'Well, not really . . .' But before I had a chance to elaborate, she had spotted an ice-cream van and had run off to buy two cones with chocolate flakes.

'That was a great idea, I really enjoyed myself,' I said, as I left Liz outside the door of her flat.

'You'd better hurry up and get ready,' she replied, 'else you'll be late.'

'Late?'

'For your show,' she said.

'Oh. Not to worry, I'm not on this week. There's a pre-Edinburgh Festival, and I'm not invited.' I sighed. 'Are you doing anything nice this evening?'

'Well, I think I'll pop across and see how my mum's doing. Surprise her, like,' said Liz.

'See you, then,' I said.

As I climbed the rest of the stairs, feeling quite relaxed and mellow after my afternoon in the sun, I decided to hire a video and spend the evening slobbing out at home. There was a message flashing on my answerphone.

Jools is right. The instant you stop thinking about the man you're involved with, he calls. Dave said that there was a band playing at the Town and Country Club, and would I be interested in going. The message relayed that he would call by at about six-thirty, which gave me all of ten minutes to shower, change and do the week's washing-up.

As I went to answer the entryphone, my arms covered in soapy suds, I spotted, in the way you do just before visitors arrive, that the kitchen rubbish bin was full and unpleasantly smelly, so I told Dave I would meet him in the pub opposite in a couple of minutes.

As it was still early he had managed to get a table outside and was sitting nursing a bottle of low-alcohol lager.

'Driving,' he said, pointing at it. 'What can I get you?'

'Something long . . . Oh, honestly,' I said, as he raised his eyebrows suggestively. 'Like two Perriers and some lime in a pint glass, please.'

'She's nice, isn't she?' he said, when he returned with my drink and some crisps.

'Who?'

'Your aunt or whatever she is.'

'What are you talking about?' I asked, opening the packet of salt and vinegar.

'At the show. Your relation,' Dave repeated slowly. 'Wakey-wakey. You know, your show, your relation.'

'I've no idea what you're talking about,' I said. 'I'm not doing a show tonight, anyway.'

He looked a bit mystified, ate a pork scratching noisily, then continued.

'I spoke to this woman at your show. She was sitting next to me. She said she came every week to see you. Said you were a relation of hers. You must know who I'm talking about.'

'When?'

'Well, I've only been once, haven't I? A couple of weeks ago.'

'What, that time I got that good-luck card? Why on earth didn't you tell me?' I said, my voice rising.

'I forgot, I suppose. It didn't seem very significant . . .'

'You didn't tell her where I lived, did you?' I interrupted.

'I can't remember. May have done, I suppose. What's the problem?'

'The problem is that apart from Mum and Reg, who are in Italy until Tuesday, I don't have any relations,' I said.

There was Reg's sister, but she had never really bothered with me much since I was her spotty bridesmaid.

'Was this person at the wedding?' I asked.

'I don't think so, but then I wasn't really looking at anyone else,' he said, leaning across the table and stroking my hand. Why is it that a twenty-eight-year-old woman with a degree and a mortgage still falls slightly to pieces when a man who hasn't called for a week says something even vaguely romantic that he has probably heard in a movie?

'Anyway, why are you telling me this now?' I said, trying to stop myself blushing.

'Because I just saw her again. I wouldn't have recognized her, but she waved,' said Dave.

'What, here?' I asked incredulously.

'Well, as I was parking, down the road.' He pointed.

'Where did she go?'

'I don't know. I thought she must have been visiting you. Are you saying you don't know who it is?'

'Towards the delicatessen, you said?'

'Yeah. I think so.'

I got up and raced down the street. The delicatessen was shutting up for the night. There was a large man with a beard paying for some Milano salami, but apart from the staff, the shop was empty. I walked back up to the pub.

'It's your fan, isn't it?' said Dave, getting up as I returned and putting his arm around me protectively. 'It's your fan. Your Annie Wilkes . . .'

'Look, don't exaggerate,' I said, although I could feel my heart beating in my head. 'What was she like?'

'Hmm. Well, she's middle-aged, I suppose. Sort of long hair.'

'Grey hair? Late middle age?' I asked.

He shrugged.

'Tall, short . . . what?' I persevered.

'Kind of average, I suppose. It's a bit difficult to say because I was in the car.'

'You're not a lot of help, are you?' I said, exasperated.

'Not really, no. No visual memory at all, according to my assessment at work. We had a security practice at work the other day. They're getting a bit jumpy about security in hospitals since that baby was snatched, you know, the one that was all over the tabloids a couple of months back. Well, we were shown videos of visitors to the ward and asked to describe them afterwards. I was absolutely useless. They're thinking of sending me on a course.' He sounded almost proud of his incompetence:

'She just waved and said hallo. She seems very nice,' he added.

'Nice? There's somebody out there who's spooking me out, and you meet her, can't remember what she looks like five minutes later, and then tell me she's nice?'

'Hey, calm down. I'm sure there's nothing to be afraid of. She looked OK, you know.'

'Just the other day, you were telling me I was about to have my legs chopped off.'

'Not really chopped off. Hobbled, Stephen King calls it.' He was teasing.

'Oh, great! Don't nurses get any training in the psychology of fear . . .' I was beginning to laugh. 'Look,' I said, 'are we going to this gig or not?'

'OK. I'm just going to powder my nose,' said Dave.

While he was gone I took a surreptitious look in my handbag mirror to see whether my hastily applied red lipstick was still in place. It was. I was putting the mirror away when I noticed a familiar figure walking up the street towards the pub. She went into the pub and came out a moment later holding a glass of water. Then she spotted a free seat and sat down, scraping the chair round on the pavement so that she could look at my building opposite.

Without really thinking about it, I got up, walked over and stood right in her line of vision.

'Hallo,' I said.

The old woman looked annoyed.

'I want to know why you're watching me,' I said calmly.

'I wasn't watching you until you got in my way,' she replied firmly.

'Yes, you were. I've seen you watching my flat several times now, and you've been talking to my boyfriend. I suspect you've also been ringing me and hanging up the phone. Why?'

'Are you mad or something?' said the woman. 'I don't even know who you are.'

I was aware that several drinkers had stopped chatting and were watching my encounter, waiting to see whether I was harassing the old dear.

'I just want to know,' I said, keeping my voice down, 'why you're taking such an interest in my affairs.'

'I'm allowed to have a glass of water without being disturbed, aren't I?' she said, raising her voice.

'I'm only trying to sort things out. I mean, if you'd just explain, I'd be less confused . . .'

'I knew there was something funny about you the first time I saw you,' she said quite nastily. 'Are you on drugs or something?'

'Something Funny?' I said. 'Did you say Something Funny?'

'Young people nowadays. They've got far too much freedom, if you ask me,' she started saying to no one in particular, but aware that she had attracted the attention of half the pub. 'All this sex and drugs and goodness knows what. In our day, we didn't know so much, you see. Now, you, young lady –' she tapped me on the shoulder – 'should mind your own business, and keep your little nose out of what doesn't concern you.'

I stepped out of her way. She folded her arms almost triumphantly. I half expected the pub audience to start clapping her, but they returned to their drinks, embar-

rassed and pretending not to have noticed the ticking-off
I had received.

Dave had caught the tail end of our conversation as he
returned from the toilets.

'Well,' he said, laughing, 'that put you in your place.
Who is that? The neighbourhood gossip?'

'It's her,' I hissed, 'the one who keeps watching me.' I
looked up at him for confirmation.

'Look, I don't want to alarm you, Sophie,' said Dave,
'but that definitely isn't the woman I saw earlier.'

I didn't really feel like going to the gig now, but Dave
insisted it would take my mind off things. Given that the
music was so loud I could hardly hear myself think, it
was a successful distraction for a few hours, but when we
left the club I immediately started thinking about the
old woman again.

'Have you got any food in?' Dave asked as we walked
down Kentish Town High Street.

''Fraid not,' I said.

'You're useless, you,' he said, only half-joking. 'I'm
starving. What do you suggest?'

There's a kebab house on the Chalk Farm Road that I
have never seen closed. Dave ordered a large doner and
chips, while I picked at some olives.

'The thing is she said "something funny" quite clearly
several times,' I said.

'Oh, you're not still going on about that, are you?'
Dave asked.

'Maybe she has seen the show and recognized herself.
Didn't you think that she talks just like my character?'

'Well, a bit, I suppose, but, Sophie, I think she is a bit
old for comedy nights in an Islington pub. You would
have noticed her there. She would have stuck out a mile.'

'But supposing I hadn't, and she was there, and she now thinks that I'm impersonating her . . .'

'That would make her a paranoid schizophrenic.'

'Is that a medical diagnosis or a horror-novel one?' I asked.

'Sophie, she's just an old woman who's a bit peculiar . . .'

I noticed that he had a slightly unattractive habit of talking with his mouth full.

'Hang on, though,' I said. 'I mean, John Lennon was killed by a fan of his, wasn't he? And Ronald Reagan, the bloke who tried to shoot him, and unfortunately missed, he said he'd been told to do it by a character in a film . . .'

'She's just an old woman, Sophie. She's hardly likely to have a Colt .45 in her handbag. And, I mean, you're a stand-up comedienne in a pub some Saturdays, not an Oscar-winning actress or . . .'

'Or the President of the United States,' I finished his sentence for him. 'Yeah, you're right. I'm sorry. But, I mean, you did see her staring, didn't you?'

'She was looking across the road, yeah. Where else was she meant to be looking?'

'But she actually turned her chair round. That's the whole point. Sorry.'

I could see Dave was getting bored with the subject and rather irritated with me.

Just my luck, I thought, that as soon as I find a nice, unattached, straightforward guy to go out with, my life turns weird.

That night we didn't even bother to make love.

Chapter Twenty

'You look terrible,' said Jools, as we emerged out of the womb-like darkness of the sauna into the brightly lit shower area.

'Thanks,' I replied. 'I didn't get much sleep.'

'Ah. Dave?'

'Yes, but not like you think,' I said.

I indicated that I didn't want to explain in the changing rooms. There was something about the all-girls atmosphere that made many of the other members blurt out the most personal of secrets to each other while showering. I had heard many intimacies swapped about thrush and late periods, as well as more mundane debates about the effectiveness of all-in-one shampoo and conditioner. I'm sure that several other club members were completely up to date with the progress of my relationship with Dave, but I didn't particularly want to broadcast my present preoccupation.

We bought some sandwiches and went and sat in the graveyard.

I tried to explain what had happened.

'Maybe it is all just my imagination,' I said. 'I mean, nothing has actually happened. I almost wish that something would, just so that I knew what was going on. Now it seems that there are two weirdos out there taking an interest in me. Do you think I'm going mad?'

'No. I don't,' said Jools.

I looked at her to see if she was joking. She wasn't.

'I mean, it all started at the bank, then Dave talks about this woman at the show who then appears in my street. Then there's the weird old woman. Perhaps they're in league. I just can't work it out. I know it sounds a bit pathetic, but I'm relieved that my mum's coming back tomorrow. I think I just might go and stay with her. I'm scared. Sounds ridiculous, but I am. Every creak the house made and every passing car woke me up last night.'

'Is Dave coming round tonight?' asked Jools.

'No,' I said. 'I think he's had quite enough of my problems. I think he's decided to take me back under the Trades Descriptions Act. I mean, he thought he was seeing a normal, healthy woman with a sense of humour, and she turns into a jibbering neurotic wreck . . .'

'Well, look, I'm not busy. I'll come over. Have you got a spare bed?'

'The sofa's pretty comfortable,' I said. 'Jools, that is incredibly nice of you. You're a real pal.'

'God, isn't he *gorgeous*?' I said as the cinema emptied. A new de Niro film had just opened at the Screen on the Hill, and we had been to see the early-evening show on the way home.

'I always forget how bloody gorgeous he is.'

'Eat your heart out, Dave,' said Jools.

'Dave who?' I asked. 'God, what I wouldn't give for a night with de Niro.'

'He's probably boring once you get talking to him,' said Jools. For some reason she wasn't entering into the girlie banter as she normally did.

'Who's talking about talking?' I said.

'D'you fancy something to eat?' Jools asked.

I couldn't really afford it, but since Jools was giving

up her evening to be with me, I decided to treat us on my credit card to a *menu du jour* at the French café next to the cinema.

Jools sipped her glass of red wine. She was in an unusually reflective mood and wasn't saying much. I get very nervous when there are long silences so I started reading the menu out loud.

'Lamb steak with a rosemary *jus*,' I read. 'Have you noticed that everything comes with a *jus* these days? Whatever happened to gravy, that's what I'd like to know? First of all it became *coulis*, or should I say *a coulis*, because some time in the late eighties a law was passed saying that you couldn't describe anything on a menu without the use of the indefinite article, then it became *a salsa*, and now it's called *a jus*. You know, I wouldn't mind betting that sometime quite soon there will be a rehabilitation of gravy. One of the Sundays will run an article called "Come back comfort food" and there'll be *a gravy* on every menu south of Watford, just like bangers and mash, except it's now called Toulouse sausages and potato purée, with *an onion jus*, of course . . .'

'God, you don't half go on,' said Jools. 'I've never heard anyone go on about food like you do.'

'Well, I've never seen anyone eat as much as you,' I countered. 'I don't know why I'm so obsessed with reading menus. It's a kind of verbal bulimia, I think. I get my kicks from reading about food, then spitting all the words out. Sad, isn't it?'

Jools looked at me oddly, then laughed, but her heart obviously wasn't in it. We ate our meal in virtual silence.

We walked back through Belsize Park and over the top of Primrose Hill. Although it was only mid-August, the nights were already getting noticeably shorter. It was almost dark by the time we approached the launderette. I glanced into the doorway of the delicatessen. There was no one there.

I noticed Jools taking a good look around as I put my key in the front door lock, and thought what a good sport she was. The bulb in the hall light had blown. We stumbled up the stairs in darkness. I was just putting my key in the door of my flat, when I heard a door opening below us. In the darkness, both Jools and I froze.

'Is that you, Sophie?' said Liz's voice.

'Yes,' I said, relieved.

'Goodnight, then,' she said.

'Goodnight,' I called, opening the door and switching on the light in my living room.

'Who's that?' said Jools.

'It's my neighbour,' I said.

'Oh, the one with the violent boyfriend?'

'Er . . . no.' I realized Jools hadn't had an update on my domestic arrangements. I told her about meeting the Stones and she laughed at my mistake about the play.

'Will they be rehearsing tonight?' she asked, eager to eavesdrop.

'No. They're in Edinburgh now,' I said, a little wistfully. This time last year I had been there too, enjoying moderate success. In the intervening year I seemed to have gone backwards.

'Do you want a drink? I think there's a can of lager,' I said.

'No. I'm fine, thanks.'

I gave Jools a tour of the flat. It was too dark to appreciate the roof terrace. Otherwise there are only two rooms and the awful avocado bathroom, so that didn't take long. We sat down in the living room and fell into an awkward silence for a moment or two. I went to the window to look out, but there was no sign of anyone looking up. I felt a bit of a fraud.

'How's your project coming along, anyway?' I asked Jools.

'What? Oh, that.' Jools seemed about to explain, then she said, 'Oh, hell, Sophie, let's have that drink after all.'

I divided a can of lager between us.

'Look . . . I don't know how to put this,' said Jools, 'but I'm not who you think I am.'

My scream must have been louder than I intended.

'I didn't mean to make you jump,' said Jools. 'Christ, I didn't realize how jittery you are.'

'I don't think I did either,' I said weakly. 'Oh, for God's sake!'

There was a loud knocking at my door.

'Sophie? *Sophie?*'

'It's all right,' I said, opening the door. 'I'm fine.'

'What's going on?'

Liz put her head inside and looked Jools up and down.

'Hallo,' said Jools.

'Hallo,' said Liz, then turned back to me. 'Whatever is the matter?' she asked.

'Jools just said something that made me jump, that's all.'

'You gave me the fright of my life,' said Liz.

'Well, I'm sorry about that,' I said, making a huge effort to remain civil.

I was eager to find out what Jools meant and my annoyance at Liz's interference was flooding back. Didn't she realize that I had lived on my own for nearly ten years, and had managed to survive without her all this time? Wasn't I allowed to raise my voice without her running upstairs? This would have to stop.

'Please leave me alone. I'm perfectly all right,' I said. 'Goodnight.'

I closed the door.

'Well?' I said to Jools. 'Go on.'

'She looks familiar,' said Jools. 'I'm sure I've met her before.'

'She's getting a bit too familiar for my liking,' I whispered. 'The soundproofing in this building is terrible and she's always checking up on me.' I was anxious to return to our conversation. 'So, as you were saying before we were so rudely interrupted . . . if you're not who I think you are, who are you?'

'The thing is, I can't really tell you,' said Jools. She was fidgeting on the oatmeal linen sofa.

'Oh, come on,' I said. This was becoming farcical. 'You're being ridiculous now.'

'No, I can't. I might lose my job. I just wanted you to know . . . Oh, hell. I'm just making things worse, aren't I?'

'Yes,' I said emphatically.

We sat in silence for a few minutes, then I had a sudden inspiration.

'How about if I guessed?' I said. 'Like a parlour game. Then if I got it right, you wouldn't have told me . . . technically.'

Jools seemed unsure. 'What, you mean like animal, vegetable or mineral?'

'Well, sort of, except I know the answer to the first, unless you're Terminator 3 or something.'

'What do you mean?'

'Animal,' I said.

'Right,' she said. 'You've got nineteen questions left.'

'Oh, that's a bit unfair. That wasn't really a question . . . Oh, all right, then.'

I was beginning to tire of the game. I had used up several questions and I didn't seem to be getting any nearer the truth. I had narrowed it down to an occupation that involved meeting people, but she wasn't a social worker. Well, she said, sometimes she felt like one. But almost everyone says that about their jobs, don't they?

'Call girl?' I said.

'Bloody hell, what a nerve. What made you think that?'

Jools shook back her long red fringe. Her lipstick was bright red, her clothes provocative. Also, I remembered, she seemed to know quite a lot about the pornography business. Her expression told me that I was getting nearer the truth.

'Yes or no answers only, remember?' I said.

'*No*,' Jools said. She looked a bit put out. 'That's nine questions you've got left.'

'God, you're taking this a bit seriously. I mean, what's it matter if I take more than nine questions? That's not the point of this particular game,' I said. Not guessing was annoying me, and, I have to admit, so was not winning.

'Rules are rules,' said Jools.

'Honestly, give me a break. Anyone would think you were a policeman!' I said, joking.

My words fell on heavy silence.

I looked up. Jools was looking back at me coolly.

'Is that a question?' she asked.

'Yes,' I stammered.

She got up, picked up her capacious black shoulder bag and extracted a wallet.

'WPC Julie Jones. Drugs Squad,' she said, flipping open her ID.

I inspected it. I had never really seen police ID before, so I didn't have the slightest idea whether it was genuine. But it looked authentic enough.

'This is a joke, right?' I said, nervously. Somehow I knew it wasn't.

'We had a tip-off that Class A drugs were being sold to staff at your bank through Eden, and we thought we knew who was responsible, but he was just a small guy and we're not interested in small guys. So I've been having a snoop around, under cover, collecting evidence, know what I mean?'

It was a relief to hear Jools's favourite catchphrase emerge from all the police-officer speak.

'Why are you telling me this now . . . Christ, you don't think I'm involved, do you?' I asked.

'I thought you were at first, popping up from nowhere, running between the bank and the gym. I mean, you didn't seem like a very body-conscious person . . . so that was a bit suspicious. But I've got to know you, and unless I'm really stupid, or you're a really good actress, I don't think you'd know one end of a joint from another, unless, of course, it was a joint of roast beef with a horseradish *jus* . . .'

I giggled. She was right. Even at university, I had never been interested in drugs. I once went out with a guy who smoked a lot of dope, but though he claimed to have profound and beautiful thoughts when he smoked, he became exceptionally boring company, unable to get further than 'Wow!' in a conversation. If that was mind-expansion, I had thought then, I could do without it. I had been offered cocaine on a couple of occasions, but it was one of those eighties things, like tequila slammers, that I had somehow never gotten round to trying.

'So far, so good, detective,' I said. 'But why are you telling me this now?'

'Well, I don't want to alarm you, but I think you may be in danger. That's why I came home with you. I'm off duty now. This isn't an official police visit . . .'

'But why . . . who?' I interrupted.

'Well, it was something you said that got me thinking. And I've been doing some checking over the weekend . . .'

The police had known that several dealers at the bank were being supplied with drugs from Eden, but the problem had stopped when the dealers and Martin's predecessor were fired. What they hadn't connected was the death of Denise, which happened very shortly after the redundancies, because that was being dealt with by a different part of the force. It was when I had suggested that Denise's death might be linked to my being followed that Jools had taken a routine look at the evidence against the guy who was in custody for the offence. Although the arresting officers thought they had a good case, there was a hole in the evidence. The murder weapon had never been found. Which meant that there was a chance that Denise had been killed by someone else. The man in custody had been found praying over her body, covered in her blood. He had confessed to her murder, but he was a deeply disturbed, former mental-hospital patient, and he might well have confessed to something he hadn't done.

'Nobody treated the death as suspicious, until you,' said Jools. 'Now we're looking into the circumstances. Turns out her boyfriend has some very dodgy connections . . . I can't tell you any more.'

'OK, OK, I understand that, but I don't see why you believe that someone's after me? I don't know anything about it. I mean, I knew that there had been a problem with drugs . . .'

Jools raised an eyebrow.

'Martin told me,' I admitted, adding, bewildered, 'But why would anyone be interested in me?'

'Well, you were the one who said someone's after you . . . It just seems too coincidental to me. That's not the official view, mind you. Call it woman's intuition, if you like. Maybe you do know something, you see, but you don't know that you know it. D'you know what I mean? Maybe they know you suspect something.'

'Yeah, but I only started suspecting something when I started getting the phone calls,' I said, trying to keep a clear head. 'I didn't suspect something, then get the phone calls.'

'Well, remember, I suspected you at first, and from what you've said about your colleagues at the bank, I wasn't the only one . . .'

Chapter Twenty-one

I desperately needed a little time on my own to think things through, in a place where I didn't jump every time a car backfired or a passer-by trod on a loose manhole cover.

I hadn't slept. Jools's presence in my flat had done little to reassure me. As well as the increasing anxiety brought about by her account of the drugs investigation, as the night wore on I also began to feel strangely betrayed by her. I had entered into our friendship in good faith, but it had been a sham all along. The confidences I had told her were genuine, those she had offered me were merely lures. I winced, remembering all the embarrassing details she knew about my past and present loves.

She was the only person I had told about the humiliation of Nat's soft-porn video. The reason she knew about the porn business, she now revealed, in the early hours of the morning, was that a couple of blokes she had done her training with were in Vice. She had mentioned Nat's activities to them, she said, and they were getting the Obscene Publications boys to look into him. She told me this as if I should be grateful. She even told me that they had discovered that Nat's main money came from importing a range of perfectly legal but rather disgusting blow-up dolls, which he stored in his so-called production office. The dolls had names like Miss Guided and Miss Tress, which was why, presumably, my stage name had such appeal to his ears.

I was appalled. As much, I have to admit, because I would have to change my stage name just when people were beginning to recognize it as because Nat's civil rights had been abused.

Jools had fundamentally and unforgivably broken the confidence that was an assumption of our friendship. She seemed to think it was sufficient compensation that she was risking her job because of our friendship. Well, I didn't agree. And people of my generation and politics weren't supposed to be friends with members of the police force, anyway.

By the morning I was feeling so cross, I showed Jools the door without even offering her a cup of coffee. She insisted on having a contact number for me. I called work. Martin wasn't in yet, I was relieved to hear. I didn't want to get into a discussion with him only to hear I was being silly. I left a message telling him where to reach me.

I put on sunglasses and a headscarf and walked towards Swiss Cottage tube station. Two nights' sleep deprivation, coupled with the knowledge that I was possibly being pursued by drugs dealers as well as batty old women, had done nothing for my nerves. I took the long route, keeping to the main roads and looking behind me constantly to see whether I was being followed. I changed tube at Finchley Road, and found myself eyeing each of my companions in the compartment suspiciously as I examined them from over the top of my *Financial Times*.

I was the only person to alight at Pinner, apart from a woman with a small child in a pushchair who had got on at Harrow-on-the-Hill. I lost her in Pinner Sainsbury's. I bought a pint of milk and a bunch of yellow roses, then headed up the road and past the church towards Mum's house. I walked past the house, stopped two doors up, then spun round to see if any people or cars were behind me. The road was empty. I ran back to Mum's house, let myself in, closed the door and stood panting in the hall. Suddenly a piercing, high-pitched whistle screamed around me. I stood frozen to the spot, my heart beating wildly. Then I remembered where the switch for the burglar alarm was located.

I turned on the hot water, put the roses in a vase in the kitchen and made myself a cup of tea. Then I went upstairs to my childhood bedroom, lay down on my single bed, with its flowery eiderdown, and fell into a blissful sleep.

'Did you forget to turn on the burglar alarm?' said Reg's voice.

'Somebody's been in, and they've had a cup of tea,' said Mum's.

I felt like Goldilocks on the return of the three bears.

'It's only me,' I shouted, jumping out of bed.

I ran down the stairs and gave Mum a great hug.

'What a lovely surprise!' she said. 'But why aren't you at work?'

In the warmth of her motherly embrace, all the emotion, anxiety and anger that I had been bottling up came welling up inside me and I burst into floods of tears.

It took a good half-hour for Mum and Reg to calm me down enough to understand what I was saying. When I managed to tell them what had been happening in the weeks since they left, they were full of concern and sympathy. Mum fetched a hot flannel from the bathroom and wiped my tear-stained eyes and runny nose, just as she had done when I was a child, and Reg hopped about trying to be useful and unobtrusive at the same time. He made some tea, which tasted funny because he had used leaves from the bottom of an ornamental tin that Mum had been given years before and hadn't wanted to throw away.

'Honestly, Reg,' said Mum, pulling a face as she sipped. 'You know I always use bags.'

She gave him a half-heartedly cross look, sighed, and went to make a fresh pot herself.

Reg winked at me.

She came back with the tea and a bag of Italian biscuits she had extracted from one of the suitcases.

'Now,' she said, practically, 'let's try to get this puzzle sorted.'

One of the best, and most used, Christmas presents I ever received from Reg was a game of Cluedo, and every year since I can remember, on Christmas Day, after the Queen's speech, we have played a game or two together.

I was reminded of this tradition as we sat outside in the garden drinking cups of tea and I gave them a résumé of the clues in the mystery I seemed to have walked into.

'So,' said Reg, 'let's just recap.' He had said this a number of times. 'In a nutshell, the situation is as follows: instead of who did what to whom with what and where, we're trying to determine who's doing what to you and why?'

'Correct,' I said. 'And, don't forget, where. There's something going on at the bank. We know that. But there was also the good-luck card at the pub.'

'And there's the old woman in your street with the patent-leather shoes,' added Mum, as if the footwear were somehow suspicious.

'Are you sure about the policewoman?' said Reg. 'She sounds a bit funny to me.'

'Funnily enough, I am pretty sure about her now,' I said. 'I saw her ID. Actually, when she told me that she wasn't who I thought she was, I wasn't *that* surprised. There were always a few things that didn't fit. Like, why was she a model if she had terrible stage fright, for instance . . .?'

'Well, she wasn't a model,' said Reg, knowingly.

'Exactly . . .' I said. 'And I just knew that her friend Frank wasn't a photographer, either. He even looked like a policeman dressed in civvies, now I come to think of it. I suppose they were trying to get a camera into the health club without the owner realizing what it was there for . . .'

'She sounds a bit silly and young to me,' said Reg. 'It's all a big adventure to her, but she's messing around with people's lives.'

'Hmm,' I said. 'Well, she is only twenty-two, I suppose. I can't believe that the police force takes people so young. God, I'm beginning to sound middle-aged! Don't they say that you know when you're growing old because the policemen all start looking young?'

'Maybe it's her first big assignment and she just got a bit carried away,' said Reg.

'Well, maybe,' said Mum. She had been silent for a while, thinking. 'I wonder if we're getting a bit side-tracked by this Jools, or whatever she's called. Now, where did you say you got the birthday card?'

I thought about it.

'It was at work.'

'I'm sure the key is the birthday card,' said Mum.

'People just don't send birthday cards on the wrong day like that. It's not a normal thing to do.'

We decided to call a time-out and Reg went in to get the drinks tray. It was a bit early in the afternoon to start drinking, but Reg felt we could all do with a little fortification. Mum and I sat beside each other in silence, rocking gently backwards and forwards on the garden seat. It had been a hot summer and the lawn was parched, but some of the standard roses were still in bloom and their scent filled the air. Here in Pinner, its tranquillity disturbed only by the distant hum of traffic and the hourly chime of the carriage clock on the mantel-piece, it was difficult to believe that anything bad could happen. I felt safe for the first time in weeks (conveniently forgetting a very bloody double murder that had hap-pened down the road about ten years before).

Mum patted my hand and stood up.

'We've brought you some presents,' she said, going inside to find them.

The soft brown leather jacket was exactly the right amount too big, and the brown leather A-line miniskirt fitted perfectly. I pulled the tissue paper out of yet another fabulously expensive-looking box to find a plain brown leather shoulder bag that matched the outfit.

'We had a weekend's shopping in Rome,' said Mum.

'But you're too generous!' I said. 'They're gorgeous, but they must have cost a fortune.'

'Oh, what's a couple of million lire here or there when you're having fun?' said Reg.

I gave him a kiss.

'Let's work back,' Mum said. She was a much more

methodical detective than Reg. I realized why, on average, she was our Cluedo champion. 'If we strip away everybody's theories, what have we got?'

She started writing a list on the message pad she usually kept by the phone.

'First of all there are the anonymous phone calls that began the day you started working at the bank.'

'Well, in the beginning they were calls for Denise,' I interrupted, 'not me. It was only after about a week that I started getting the silences, then it was a while before she began speaking.'

'Right,' said Mum, writing BANK in brackets beside CALLS.

'Now, what happened next? You get a good-luck card and a birthday card. Were you still getting the telephone calls at this stage?'

I thought hard.

'I don't think so.'

'So, she, whoever it is, switches from verbal to written communication.'

'Sounds like *Close Encounters of the Third Kind*,' said Reg, humming the five-note tune from the film.

'Oh, do be quiet. I'm trying to concentrate. I don't think we ought to bring an extraterrestrial element in at this stage, do you?' said Mum.

I suppressed a laugh. Mum could be inadvertently very witty at times.

'Now, both cards have the same handwriting on, and you got one at the pub. That's the first communication at the pub, as far as we know. And the birthday card arrived at the bank, soon after, so there's a definite link between the pub and the bank.'

She drew a double arrow between the words PUB and BANK.

'Now, you say you've had calls at home, but we don't know that for certain, because the caller didn't speak, right?'

I began to protest, but I knew that she was right.

'What else has happened at home?' Mum asked. 'Well, there's the old woman across the road. There must be some explanation for that . . . Let's just suppose that the old woman is the same one who is calling you. Why would she deny it when confronted?'

'I think she might be a bit batty,' I said. 'Although she looks fine.'

'Then there's the woman that Dave saw in Islington and in your street,' contributed Reg. 'She's the link between the pub and your home. It's that woman that we're after. *Cherchez la femme*, as they say.'

'But did that woman send the cards or make the calls?' asked Mum.

'Well, that's it, in a nutshell, isn't it? No lemon, I'm afraid,' said Reg, pouring us all a gin and tonic.

'And what about the drugs aspect?' I interjected.

'No. Apart from Jools's theory, you have no reason to think that that is anything to do with you,' said Mum. 'It might just be a red herring.'

I knew I could rely on her to be calm, but for all the diagrams and flow charts she had etched on the message pad, we were no nearer to solving the mystery.

'What about other witnesses?' said Mum, trying a new line of inquiry. 'There's the receptionist. If we believe her, and on balance we do, then the calls must be coming from outside the building where you work, because if they were coming from inside they wouldn't go through her.'

'Yes, but that hardly narrows it down, does it?' I said.

'Also, they record all the calls, you told us,' said Reg. 'Couldn't you ask Martin to get you a tape so that we could listen for clues?'

'That's a brilliant idea, Reg,' said Mum. 'Go and ring him up, Soph.'

'He'll have left work by now,' I said, looking at my watch. 'I'll ring him tomorrow.'

I didn't relish the prospect of asking Martin for the tapes. I was virtually sure that he wouldn't have security clearance for them anyway, and it would look very suspicious if he was caught borrowing them for me secretly.

'What about your neighbours? Have they noticed anything funny?' asked Mum.

'I haven't seen Elena for a while, and you know how Costas always gets the wrong end of the stick . . . I don't like the others much. Did I tell you about meeting them?'

I told them about my encounter with the Stones.

'And then there's my new neighbour, Liz, but I'm not discussing it with her. She's becoming a bit of a nightmare, actually.'

I described her intervention the previous evening.

'Oh, you are hard, Sophie,' said my mother. 'The poor woman's only trying to be nice and friendly.'

'Anyway,' I said, 'all this started long before she moved in.'

We had come to another dead end.

We sipped in silence.

'What time of day did you say the calls came through?' said Mum.

I was beginning to feel that Mum had missed her vocation as a forensic investigator.

'It's a long time since I've had one, but usually there was one in the morning about eleven, often one before I went to lunch, and one as I was packing up to go home. There were often more on Monday than any other day.'

'Well, that sounds to me like someone who's calling from work,' said Mum. 'She makes one call in her morning coffee break, one at lunch, one when she clocks off. But why? Doesn't she have a phone at home? What makes her unable to call from home?'

'Well, she doesn't have Sophie's home number, as far as we know, so she can only call her in work hours,' suggested Reg.

'You're right, darling,' said Mum. 'I thought I was making a breakthrough then.'

'What about the frequency of Monday calls?' asked Reg. 'Maybe that's because she's seen the show. There's a link now.'

'Yes, but we've already got the link between the show and the bank, Reg,' said Mum patiently. 'The cards.' She pointed to the message pad with the arrows drawn between the pub and the bank. 'Why would anyone send a birthday card on the wrong day? They would only do that if they were convinced that it was your birthday. Otherwise why would they think of it?'

My head was beginning to spin again. I drained my gin and tonic.

'Let's talk about something else for the moment,' I said.

We were all silent for a few minutes, then Reg said, 'So, you've seen my friend Dave again, have you?'

I blushed.

'Well, yes, but before you start speculating, I don't think it's anything serious,' I said.

I was saved from further embarrassment by the telephone ringing.

Reg got up to answer it.

Mum smiled a little conspiratorial smile at me, which said that she'd like to hear all the details about my new relationship later. I heard Reg saying, 'Yes, she's here.'

Mum stood up to go and take the call, then Reg shouted, 'Sophie . . . it's for you.'

'Hallo?' I said cheerfully.

There was a familiar silence. I started shaking. Then the voice said, 'Is that you, Sophie? Are you all right?'

'Look, who is this?' I said, but even as I asked the question I knew the answer. 'Why are you calling? How did you get my number?' I wanted to keep her talking so that I could be absolutely sure.

'I rang the bank, of course. I spoke to Martin. He seems very nice. He said you'd be at this number.'

It was definitely the same voice as before. Why hadn't I realized? Well, first of all because she didn't look anything like the dumpy middle-aged woman with a perm that I always envisaged. I had to keep her talking.

'Why are you calling?' I repeated.

'I've been so worried about you. You might have told me you were going away, you know. I've called your home number all day but I keep getting that silly answerphone.'

'How did you get my home number, as a matter of fact?' I asked as casually as I could. She hadn't been inside my flat and I certainly hadn't given her the number.

'Oh, Costas has all our numbers listed in his kitchen. Look, Sophie, are you sure everything's all right? After all that screaming last night, I just didn't know what to do.'

'I'm fine,' I reassured her. 'Where are you?' I asked as the pips started going, indicating that she was in a phone box.

'I'm calling from work.'

'Are you going home now?' I asked.

'Yes.'

'Well, I'll see you later, then,' I said.

'Oh, are you coming back tonight? I'll get us some supper.'

'Don't bother,' I said.

'It's no trouble,' said Liz happily, just before the line went dead.

As soon as I put the phone down it rang again. I snapped it up.

'Yes?'

'Oh, is that you, Sophie?' said Jools's London accent.

'Yup.'

'You OK?'

'Yup.'

I was in no mood to chat to her.

'Look, I was just calling to see if you were OK. Know what I mean?'

'Yeah. Look, Jools, I'm fine.'

'And I thought you might like to know. I figured out where I'd seen that neighbour of yours before.'

I braced myself. Visions of Jools at a police station flipping through books of photo-fit pictures of serial killers flooded my mind.

'You know when I came to see your show, that first time, you know, the Roberta Flat evening?'

'Yeah, I know the one you're talking about.'

'She was there, in the audience. She said she knew you, or was related, or something.'

'And I suppose you told her where I worked?' I said, slotting in another piece of the jigsaw.

This was the final connection. Jools had come to the show the first weekend after I met her. Which was also the first weekend after I started at the bank. I remembered that particularly, because I had been delighted at the time to have found a friend at work so quickly. Now, I thought with some bitterness, I knew that her eagerness to find out about me and my show was just a cover. She was simply putting in a bit of overtime. But if she had talked to Liz there, that explained how Liz had found out where I worked. It was ironic, I thought, that the undercover cop had in fact given away the one piece of information that led my pursuer to me.

'I can't remember whether I did tell her,' Jools was saying. 'We had a little chat. I suppose I could have done. Why d'you ask?'

Chapter Twenty-two

'Why?'

I don't know how many times we all said that word in Reg's Rover on the way into central London.

Why hadn't I connected the voice on the telephone with that of my new neighbour? Well, as well as having a flat, ordinary voice, the only reason I could come up with was that the calls had stopped before she moved in. So I had never really had a chance, or reason, to compare her telephone voice with her voice in person. After all, she didn't need to talk to me on the phone when she could chat to me over breakfast in the patisserie. And perception has a lot to do with expectation. I hadn't dreamt that the person who was pursuing me could be so close.

But that led to the bigger why. Why on earth was this apparently mild-mannered woman taking such an interest in me and my welfare? An interest that was beginning to look like an obsession. She had followed me from my show, via the bank, to my home, and now she had installed herself underneath my flat, where she could listen to everything I did and said. There was something very funny about that.

We picked Dave up at Northwick Park. I now felt sure that he would confirm Jools's identification of Liz as the mystery relation. I couldn't believe that I had been so dumb.

'Don't punish yourself, Soph,' Reg said comfortingly. 'I mean, it's not normal what you've been through, you know.'

Why, Dave asked, had Liz said that she was a relation of mine, rather than a friend or neighbour?

'Well, she wasn't my neighbour when Jools met her,' I explained.

'But she's not a relation, either,' said Mum sensibly.

As usual, there was nowhere to park in Regent's Park Road. Reg dropped Mum and me on the corner, by the pub, and he and Dave drove off, looking for a space. Dave had wanted to get out, too, but I felt safe enough with Mum, and I didn't want to intimidate Liz or send her into a panic. If we hadn't emerged from Liz's flat within ten minutes, we agreed with the boys, they would intervene. We synchronized our watches.

Mum held my hand firmly as we strode purposefully towards the front door. The street was busy: cars double-parked, with their lights flashing, waiting for their drivers to return after picking up bags of home-made pasta from the delicatessen, or clean washing from the launderette; taxis bringing people home; the inevitable truck blocking the road as it unloaded outside the off-licence. Most of the tables outside the pub were already full, and there was a queue at the patisserie. Two doors down towards the park, outside the picture-framer's shop, I spotted Liz in conversation with another person.

I stood still for a moment, holding Mum's hand tightly.

'There she is,' I said to Mum and nodded towards the frame shop.

Mum gave my hand a squeeze for courage and we stepped out together towards her.

*

As we drew nearer I began to pick out voices over the sound of traffic.

'Just leave me alone, will you?' said Liz.

'You can't be left alone, that's your problem. We never could leave you alone. You get yourself into trouble. You were the ruin of yourself, and us.'

'Well. I've left you now. You should be glad. So why do you keep following me, eh?' Liz's voice rose. 'Just leave me alone,' she repeated.

'You want your head seeing to, you do. Who do you think you are, living in this part of London, a two-bedroom flat indeed. You'll never keep up the rent, you know. Then they'll throw you out. Then you'll come crawling back to me,' the older woman hectored on. I recognized her voice too.

'No, I won't,' said Liz. 'I can look after myself,' she added slightly uncertainly.

'What's going on, Liz?' I said gently, drawing closer.

The older woman turned round, her spectacles flashing in the last rays of sunshine.

'You again,' she said huffily. 'Mind your own business, will you?'

'No, I won't,' I replied defiantly. 'Hallo, Liz. Are you all right?'

I noticed that Liz had frozen. She was staring at my mum with a look of sheer bewilderment on her face.

'Hallo, Sophie,' she said eventually.

'Sophie, is it? Oh, that explains it, that does. It's all becoming clear now, isn't it?' the older woman started shouting, her face right next to Liz's ear. 'So that's what this is all about, is it?'

Liz cowered away from her.

'Leave her alone,' I said.

Mum gripped my hand. I could tell she was frightened. It was becoming an ugly scene.

Then Liz started sobbing. 'Yeah, Mum, leave me alone. Leave me alone. Leave me alone!'

She turned away from us, her face against the shop window, her fists above her head pounding ineffectually at the glass.

The older woman, Mum and I looked at her, not knowing what to do.

'You're Liz's mother?' I finally asked the older woman in disbelief.

She nodded, obviously taken aback by her daughter's distress.

'This is my mother,' I said, pulling Mum forward.

Liz suddenly quietened. She stopped sobbing almost as quickly as she had started. She stood up straight and wiped her eyes, and as she did she caught a glimpse of the three of us watching her in the large, gold-framed mantel mirror on display in the window.

I saw the tableau as she was seeing it. On the far right, there was my mum, still wearing her navy-blue cotton travelling trousers and flat shoes; next to her me, with exactly the same colour hair, looking as ever like a scruffier version of Mum, with my frayed blue jeans and plimsolls. Next to me was Liz's mum, a grey-haired, bespectacled and more robust version of herself.

'Oh dear,' Liz said quietly. 'Mum, I've done it again, haven't I?'

And she began to wail, softly at first, then louder, until a terrible, terrified scream emerged and she started shaking involuntarily.

We managed to coax Liz and her mother up to my flat. Dave had the presence of mind to call a doctor, who gave her a mild sedative and decided, after a whispered conversation with her mother, to admit her to hospital for observation. Reg offered to drive them there. I sat in the back with Liz, trying to comfort her.

Her mother was sitting on the other side of the back seat. She was tight-lipped and reluctant to explain anything, even under the gentlest of interrogations by my mum.

Liz began to breathe more normally and her sobbing subsided. I felt she wanted to talk, to explain, but she wasn't very coherent.

All I could work out from the brief snatches of sentence she managed to get out between icy reprimands from her mother was that she seemed to be suffering from some kind of delusion about my identity.

'But you look just like her. You look just like her,' she kept saying, pointing at the front passenger seat. 'And you don't look at all like me.'

Chapter Twenty-three

It was only when I paused and looked down at the three empty coffee cups in front of me that I realized how long I must have been talking. The waiter scooped up the brimming ashtray and asked pointedly if there was anything else. I ignored him.

'Liz had convinced herself that I was her daughter, you see,' I said to Charlotte.

I watched carefully for her reaction.

She lit another Gauloise and inhaled thoughtfully. I found her coolness quite disconcerting. Blue smoke and silence hung between us.

'At first it freaked me out a lot,' I said, chattering on nervously. 'To be honest, I didn't want to think about it. Liz's mother obviously wanted to brush everything under the carpet and I was happy to blank it all out too. She came and took Liz's few possessions away from the flat and paid Costas the rent for the rest of the lease.'

My life had returned to normal. I went on working at the bank. I even met Jools in the sauna at Eden one lunchtime and got chatting. Our friendship wasn't the same, but we were able to have a good laugh about our misunderstandings. She said that her assignment had finished and she was doing a desk job now. I didn't know whether to believe her or not.

I didn't give Liz much thought until Mum and Reg popped in one evening on their way home from a musical.

As we sat on my roof terrace, eating ice-cream that they had picked up from Marine Ices, we were treated to a strenuous love scene from Jonathan Stone's new play, and to cover his embarrassment at the intimate noises that were floating up, Reg asked whether I had heard from Liz. I said that I hadn't, and that I was beginning to miss her, because the woman who had moved into her flat had a baby who had not yet started sleeping through the night. At least Liz had been quiet, I said.

After they left, I felt a bit guilty for being so glib. In the brief time that I had known her, Liz had always been kind to me, and, apart from her taste in greetings cards, she seemed like a nice person. Now I knew that she had been the mystery caller, I wasn't frightened. As the days went by, I wondered how I ever could have been.

I couldn't get the image of her sobbing against the window of the frame shop out of my mind. I rang her mother and asked if I could speak to her. She told me that Liz was still in hospital. She was perfectly all right, she said. And no, she didn't want any visitors. She banged down the phone with her customary grace.

It didn't seem fair. Liz hadn't done anything wrong, really. I hated the thought of her imprisoned in a psychiatric ward or, worse, at home with her domineering mother. One evening, on my way to a friend's thirtieth-birthday bash, I found myself walking quite near the hospital, so I popped in.

I don't think that she had many friends, or else they hadn't been told where to find her. Her mother had been advised by the doctors not to visit for a while, so I think she was quite lonely. The first few times I went to see her we talked about trivial things. I would describe my day at the bank, or perform a little bit of my latest character for her (I had dropped Something Funny, and now called myself plain Sophie Fitt). She would tell me about a book she was reading. She read a lot. Gradually, we built up a kind of trust. Once she felt that I had forgiven her for inadvertently frightening me, she started talking to me about her life and I began to piece her story together.

She had become pregnant when she was fourteen. She was so sheltered and innocent that she hadn't even known what she was doing. By the time they discovered that she was pregnant, she was virtually about to have the baby. It was still a scandal in those days. The swinging sixties hadn't made much impression on her little home town. Elizabeth (she had been named after the new queen – that's the sort of people her parents were) was shipped off to a nursing home and an adoption society contacted.

'She can't remember a lot about that time, except that her baby was a little girl, and she called it Sophia, after Sophia Loren. The father of the child was Italian. He was the son of the town's ice-cream-van owner. They had been childhood sweethearts as they grew up together, but then he seems to have grown up a little faster than she did.

'Liz isn't sure, but she thinks her father drove her boyfriend and his family out of town while she was in the nursing home. Anyway, she has never seen him again.

'She remembers them taking the baby away after a couple of weeks. She was a minor, and the matter was literally taken out of her hands. She never met the adopting parents. All she can remember is her mother saying that the baby would be well looked after, and something about doctors in Norwich . . . as if the baby were really lucky to have gone up in the world.'

I looked up. Charlotte met my gaze, but her hands were shaking as she tapped another Gauloise from its blue packet. I picked up the book of matches and lit her cigarette for her. I thought it was important to continue talking.

'Once the baby had been effectively disposed of, they brought Liz home, and life was supposed to continue as normal. The baby was never mentioned. Liz says that sometimes she wondered whether it had ever happened at all. I think that the cover-up was the root of all Liz's problems.'

I began to realize that talking to me was helping Liz, enabling her to release some of the memories she had suppressed for years. Her treatment involved an appointment with a psychiatrist once a day, but she only saw him for an hour, and I just knew that there were some things she would only tell a woman. I tried to make an appointment with the psychiatrist to ask his advice. It worried me that I wasn't trained to help Liz, and I wondered whether he would be able to give me a few tips. I received a curt note back from him saying that he couldn't possibly discuss his confidential relationship with his patient. I thought it an arrogant response, so I decided to try another tactic. I rang my friend Stephanie and asked if she could recommend a therapist I could talk to.

'I'm so pleased that you've acknowledged your problem,' said Stephanie, after giving me a number. 'I'm sure she will help you.'

'Actually, it's not for me, it's for a friend,' I said.

'Hmm. Perhaps you've got a bigger problem than I thought with denial,' said Stephanie.

I couldn't be bothered to put her right.

But the therapist she recommended was very helpful and, while she couldn't provide any answers, she recommended a couple of books to read, and explained how one might begin hypothetically to interpret Liz's problem.

She also asked me a number of probing and insightful questions about why I was taking such an interest. I ended up seeing her a few times, talking about my own feelings of abandonment by my father. Talking did help, I realized, because I always left her house feeling better than when I arrived. My resolve to meet my own father strengthened.

'What I can't understand is why this Liz thought that you were her child,' said Charlotte.

'It took us a while to work out too. She couldn't explain it at first,' I said. 'Then one night I went up to the pub in Islington and I happened to notice the 73 bus going past with Stoke Newington written on the front as its destination. Well, one of my friends lives in Stoke Newington and I know it's in the borough of Hackney, where Liz used to live, and the route goes all the way down Oxford Street, so I asked Liz how she got to work every morning. Sure enough, she said the 73 bus. So, every morning she would be sitting on the bus in a traffic jam, you see, and she would see my picture and my name on those posters. She says that one day she just found herself at my show, and she happened to talk to Jools, who happened to tell her where I worked. So she started calling me, and coming to the show, and one week she bumped into Dave, who mentioned Primrose Hill. Well, it's not a very big place, and when she saw the flat to rent, she thought she was destined to live near me. She didn't even realize then that I lived in the flat right above her.'

'So, she thought you were her daughter just because you had the same first name?' asked Charlotte. 'I don't believe that.'

'I'm not asking you to,' I said, quite crossly. 'It's probably much more complex than that. There would have been various triggers, my friendly psychologist says. The character Something Funny being rather like her mother might have made Liz think that I was related to her. My age is about right too. There's no way of saying definitively what sends someone off balance, and when it happened before, she was treated with drugs that probably didn't really help . . .'

'What do you mean, it happened before?' Charlotte interrupted quickly.

She was extremely sharp. I kicked myself for letting this information out so soon. This was the bit I hadn't really wanted to tell, just yet. It would be difficult enough for Charlotte to picture Liz as a sympathetic character, although I had tried my best to make her seem as nice and unthreatening as possible, but this bit of the story did make her sound genuinely loopy. I took a deep breath.

'Everything looked as if it was fine after the baby was adopted. Liz went back to school, got some O-levels, became a nurse. Nobody knew what had happened. She was twenty, still living at home, but doing well at work, getting promotion and all that. Her parents were really proud of her. She was about to become a sister on the children's ward, when a little girl was admitted to the hospital with appendicitis. She was called Sophia. The other nurses noticed that Liz became unusually attached to this little girl, so when the child disappeared two days before she was supposed to be discharged from the hospital, they remarked on this fact to the investigating officer.

The police found the little girl in the storeroom at the back of Liz's parents' shop. She was perfectly happy, because she was surrounded by all the sweets she could eat. She hadn't been there very long, and nobody knows what Liz was planning to do with her, but she was charged with abducting the child.'

'That's why they had to leave and come to live in London . . . That's why her mother was so frightened for her . . .' said Charlotte.

'Yes. And that's why they've overprotected Liz ever since. The judge sent her for a spell in a mental hospital. Liz doesn't have any memory of it. When she eventually got out, she couldn't go back to nursing, obviously, so she got a job under the eye of her domineering father. And she always felt that she had ruined his life. The psychologist I spoke to thought his recent death might be another trigger for her going adrift again.'

'Poor woman,' said Charlotte.

I heaved a huge sigh of relief. I had been expecting one of two reactions from her – fear or sympathy. I was so pleased that she had chosen sympathy. Once you knew her, Liz was pretty hard to fear.

'So,' said Charlotte, 'Liz is my mother.'

I nodded.

We sat in silence for a few minutes. Charlotte stirred spoonful after spoonful of sugar into her third camomile tea, until I put my hand on hers to stop her.

'Thanks,' she said, and a great tear slid down her face.

I left her to her own thoughts and went to the washroom. By the time I returned, she had regained her ice-cool composure.

Chapter Twenty-four

'What I still don't understand,' she said, 'is how you found me. I've known ever since I can remember that I was adopted, and occasionally I wondered who my mother was and why she gave me away. I know that I'm allowed by law to see my original birth certificate, but you have to get counselling before you do, and I've just never wanted to go into all of that, especially while my parents are alive. They are my parents,' she added firmly, seeing the flicker of surprise cross my face. 'It's more than just biology, you know.'

I nodded.

'Of course I know that,' I said. 'Reg has been a better father to me than most natural fathers have ever been to their daughters.'

'So how did you know where to find me?' repeated Charlotte.

'I just got this idea in my head that Liz wouldn't be as likely to go off the rails again if she knew that her daughter was safe. I asked her whether she had ever looked for her, but she had been told – by her parents, I suppose – that it was illegal for mothers to search for their children. Privately, I thought she must have been misled. I rang up the local social services and they confirmed what I thought. They told me that it wasn't illegal, just very difficult. The thing was, I didn't want to get Liz's hopes up. I had to find a way of finding you without her being involved. She doesn't know I'm here,' I added quickly.

'I was never sure whether I was doing the right thing . . .' I looked at Charlotte's face for encouragement.

'I don't know yet,' she said, understanding my unspoken demand.

'I had long conversations with this therapist about it, but naturally she didn't want to express an opinion one way or another. She did say when I pressed her that she thought that in an ideal world it would be good for Liz to know that her daughter was safe. The only other person I spoke to about it was Dave. He'd had some experience of dealing with mental health and I knew he would tell me honestly what he thought. Well, he said that it wasn't an ideal world. He thought I was trying to play God. He asked some pretty uncomfortable questions.'

'Like?'

'Like, what if I found you and you turned out to be a drug addict or something,' I blurted out.

That was what finally ended my relationship with Dave. We had a bit of a row. If truth be told, I didn't really want his honest opinion if it turned out to be different from mine. I accused him of interfering. He responded, with a particularly annoying chuckle, that if anyone was interfering, it wasn't him. It was the sort of quarrel about nothing that you have when a relationship is on its way out. We decided to call it a day before it became acrimonious.

I sometimes wonder what would have happened if we had met at a different time. I remember how I was that first day, sitting next to Reg's bed and making everyone laugh. I remember the intensely erotic moment of anticipation before he first kissed me, and I remember that idyllic weekend on the Isle of Wight. There had been something special going on there, but for some reason, neither of us had really grabbed at it, and after that it just seemed to melt away.

At least we managed to finish on good enough terms. He came along to my last show at the pub. Jools was there too. They seemed to be getting on so well, they hardly noticed when I left to go home and pack.

'At least I'm not a drug addict,' said Charlotte. 'However, I could do with a drink.'

We ordered two glasses of kir.

'I didn't have very much to go on,' I continued. 'If I had known at the beginning that I had only one chance of finding you, I don't think I would have bothered. But once I had started looking, the investigation took on a momentum of its own. It's like doing a jigsaw, except it's more three-dimensional than that – more like one of those logic exercises, where you have certain pieces of information that you think tell you nothing, but if you put them in the right order and eliminate possibilities, then you end up with a larger picture.'

Charlotte was now sitting forward, interested. I noted that she was happier dealing with games of logic than with emotions.

When I first went to St Catherine's House, I imagined that there would be more information available. In fact, the huge, heavy volumes containing the records of adoption give only the adoptive name of the child, the year in which the child was born and the date that the name was entered into the register. Not the original name, not the date of birth, no indication of the place where the adoption took place.

'I was lucky that your adoption took place in the early sixties. In later years, they just put the child's year of birth, making it all the more difficult to whittle down the numbers.'

'How many people are adopted each year, then?' asked Charlotte.

I told her that in the year of her adoption there were well over 100 pages. Each page had two columns of about forty names each, making a total of about 8,000 names.

'And they're all typed higgledy-piggledy on an old-fashioned typewriter,' I added. 'You can only check a few pages at a time because your head starts swimming.'

'But surely they're arranged alphabetically?' said Charlotte.

'Yes, but that doesn't help if you don't know the surname, does it?' I responded.

'Sorry,' she said.

After spending several lunch hours poring over the names, hoping inspiration would leap out of the page, I asked the clerk what the significance of the date of entry into the register was. He told me that it was usually between two days and six weeks after the court hearing – that is, the actual adoption.

'Well, I knew your birthday.'

Charlotte looked perplexed.

'It was a matter of remembering which day the birthday card arrived at the bank.'

'Oh, of course, the card. So, your mother was right about its significance,' she said.

'So I just wrote down all the girls' names that fell for about six weeks after that in the year. Since your birthday's in July, I wrote all the names that fell in July, August and September, because Liz had told me that you were adopted more or less straight away.'

'That's amazing. When did you do all this?' asked Charlotte.

'Mostly in my lunch hours. It became a bit of an obsession. I hate being beaten by the system. I mean, why do they make it so difficult, for heaven's sake? Why shouldn't this woman, whose whole life has been mucked up by the fact that she got pregnant when she was an adolescent, have access to information that might make her change her life? Sorry . . .' I broke off. 'It's become a bit of a moral crusade for me, I'm afraid.'

'No, don't be sorry. You're right. I've just never thought of it like that. I've always thought of my mother as the person who rejected me, didn't want me . . . Go on. I'm interested.'

After about four weeks spending every lunch hour in the busy Public Record Office, I had a list of about 400 names. I was stuck. The only other piece of information I had was that the child's adoptive parents had been doctors. It would have been possible, I suppose, to buy copies of the certificates of adoption of all 400 children. The full certificates, I discovered, give the place of adoption. There can't have been that many people in East Anglia adopting at that particular time, so it would have taken me a step further. I was sure that there must be registers of doctors I could get hold of and match the surnames against once I had narrowed down the list to a few names in that area. The trouble was that the full certificates cost £5.50 each, and I didn't have £2,000 to spare. I also thought that the staff at St Catherine's House might think me a bit odd.

I couldn't see a way of getting further. I stared and stared at the names. There seemed to be dozens of Patricias and Karens and Lorraines. Very few people seemed to choose unusual Christian names in those days. Even Sophia, I noticed, wasn't at all common. In fact there were only two in my list. Both second names.

I remembered Liz telling me early on that Sophia was the name on her daughter's birth certificate. Perhaps, I thought in desperation, the adoptive parents had respected the mother's wishes.

'So I decided on a hunch to buy the adoption certificates of both Sophias and one of them turned out to be you. I can't tell you what a feeling of triumph I got when I looked at the second adoption certificate and realized, Charlotte Sophia, that I'd found you.'

'But you hadn't found me. You'd found my adoption certificate.'

'Yes, but it's incredibly easy to trace someone from that, especially when her parents are GPs and have only moved once since she was born. There was a slight hiccup, though.'

There are lists of GPs in town halls, so I went up to Norwich to look at the archives. The surname wasn't there. That was a real blow. I tried the hospital records too. No luck. I thought I had come to the end of the trail. But by this time I had invested so much energy in the whole enterprise, I just couldn't let it go.

'Well, this is where I got a bit devious. The only person I knew definitely would have had the information I wanted was Liz's mum. But I knew from previous experience that she wouldn't speak to me.' I hesitated, wondering whether I should reveal all to Charlotte. But I had gone so far, I couldn't really stop now. I took a deep breath.

'So I had to pretend not to be me. I'm quite good at putting on voices. I thought about it for a long time and rehearsed. Eventually I rang her up, pretending to be a stroppy official from the East Anglian social services department. I knew she was the sort of person who would respect authority. I told her that we were putting the adoption records on to computer, but that some of our information was missing. I ran through the details I had on the adoption certificate, so she thought I was genuine, and then I asked about the adoptive parents. "Dr and Mrs — from Norwich, right?" I said. "No," she said. "They were from Ipswich." Bingo!'

'So you've spoken to my parents?' said Charlotte.

'No,' I replied. 'Well, yes. But they didn't know who I was. I'm afraid that I lied when I spoke to your mum. She was very helpful actually. She made it very easy for me.'

I had felt a bit rotten about it at the time. I rang and told her that I was a friend of Charlotte's who had lost touch.

'From university?' she'd asked.

'Yes,' I agreed, hoping that she would lead me further.

'Oh, yes, I'm sure I remember Charlotte talking about you,' she said politely.

She gave me a résumé of Charlotte's postgraduate studies and her phone number.

'And, well, when I found out you were studying in Paris, it seemed fated that we should meet,' I said, draining my glass of kir. 'The symmetry of me finding my father and you finding your mother was too potent to resist. So I quit work and I finally came to Paris. So here we are . . .'

My story petered out. I looked over the table hopefully for her reaction.

*

'You've gone to an awful lot of trouble,' she finally said. 'I wish I could just say yes, I'd love to meet my real mother, thank you very much. But I can't. I've got to think it all through.'

My face must have fallen, because she quickly added, 'I am very grateful to you. I've really enjoyed meeting you, too. But you have to understand, it's a bit weird for me.'

I could see why she was at the Sorbonne doing post-graduate studies in philosophy. She understood complex things immediately, but took a reasoned, considered approach.

I couldn't hide the fact that I was terribly disappointed. I wanted her to be impulsive and excited, to order a bottle of champagne and drink to reunited families. Instead she gathered up her cigarettes and handbag, started peeling on her gloves, and called the waiter over to pay the bill.

We walked a little way down the street together.

'There may be things I need to ask you,' she said. 'May I call you?'

'Of course,' I said.

We parted at the Métro.

I went back to my father's apartment and got exceedingly drunk with him and his lover. At three in the morning we all came to the conclusion that she was an ungrateful, unimaginative, stuck-up cow who would be better off learning a bit about life than studying philosophy.

Chapter Twenty-five

I woke up to the ringing of the phone. I dragged myself off the sofa and into the kitchen. There was a note propped against an empty bottle of Calvados saying that my father and his lover had gone shopping. They were inviting a nice young man to dinner, it said, and I should wear something alluring. I smiled and picked up the phone.

'Sophie. It's Charlotte. I'm ringing to apologize. You must have thought me terribly rude.'

'Not at all,' I said, crossing my fingers.

'Could we have lunch?' she asked.

The weather had become colder and there was ice on the pavements. Charlotte had suggested a small café in a tiny street off the Boulevard Montparnasse which was obviously frequented by students and artists, but rather difficult to find. I was half an hour late.

The tables were covered in plain white paper, and there was a pot of crayons to doodle with in the centre of each in place of a vase of flowers. Charlotte looked up from her drawing of a sprig of holly and smiled at me. Only the evening before my father had been telling me that Picasso used sometimes to pay his bills by sketching on the tablecloth. Glancing at Charlotte's efforts, I hoped that she had some more conventional means of paying.

She got up and kissed me on both cheeks.

'I'm so relieved,' she said. 'I thought, after my performance yesterday, you had decided not to come.'

'No, I just got lost,' I said, feeling rather guilty for having been so horrible about her. She seemed very keen to be friendly and I mentally retracted all the bad things I had said about her.

'I've been thinking a lot,' Charlotte began, 'as you can imagine, and there are so many things I want to ask.'

We chatted over cassoulet and a bottle of red wine. I suspected that Charlotte may have spent the night drinking too, since she looked pretty grim and she got a little tipsy after only one glass. She was much more relaxed and giggly than she had been the day before. When she laughed she had dimples, like her mother. I began to warm to her.

I told her, as best I could, what she wanted to know. We drank coffee after coffee as the light faded outside and the streetlamps came on.

Towards the end of my explanation, I noticed that Charlotte had become quiet and reflective. I stopped talking.

'Do you think Liz would . . .?' she asked very nervously.

'Would what?'

'W-w-would l-l-like me?' she stuttered.

'What?' I couldn't believe that someone who appeared so cool and sophisticated on the outside could doubt herself so obviously. 'She'd love you. Of course she would.'

'Really? You're not just saying that?'

'Really,' I said.

She took a deep breath.

'OK, then,' she said finally. 'I think I'd better meet her. I'm spending Christmas with my parents. Maybe after that?'

'That's wonderful! She'll be so happy, honestly,' I said, scribbling down an address in thick blue crayon on the tablecloth and tearing it off. 'Look, could you do me a favour?' I asked, handing over the piece of paper.

'I think I owe you one,' said Charlotte.

'Could you tell her that you were looking for her and leave me out of it? It's only a little lie, but it would make it so much easier for her. And,' I had to admit, 'for me.'

'Of course I will,' said Charlotte. 'At least I know how I would have gone about it now. I think I can manage to sound authentic. She's moved back to Primrose Hill, then?' she added, looking at the piece of paper.

'Yes. She's renting my flat, while I'm away. She couldn't go back to living with her mother. At least Costas and Elena can keep an eye on her. And my plants will get watered.'

'What about you?' she asked, as we slithered down the Boulevard Montparnasse together, stopping occasionally to look at the Christmas windows. 'What are you going to do? Are you going back to work at the bank?'

'No, I've finished there. Thank God,' I said. I started giggling.

'What?' she said, giggling too.

'Well, on my last day, Martin called me in and asked if I'd mind getting lunch in for the boys in the dealing room because they were expecting a mad rush when New York opened, and he didn't want them having to go out for lunch. So I went out and got tons of sandwiches from Marks and Spencer and spent the morning making little flags out of cocktail sticks and multicoloured Post-it notes, with "cheese and celery", "chicken tikka with yog-hurt and mint", etc., written on them. It was much appreciated by the boys, so much appreciated, in fact, that there was nothing left for me. I couldn't nip out because things were getting lively, but I was starving.

Then I remembered the sachets of instant soup in my desk drawer.

'I didn't really look at the powder until I poured the boiling water on, but then I saw that it wasn't pale green with croutons, as suggested on the packet, but pure white . . . I had just poured boiling water on about 1,000 quid's worth of coke. Jools and her team had got it wrong. Coke wasn't coming from Eden to the bank: it was the other way round. Denise, or probably her boyfriend, was a major dealer. No wonder she had been so popular. The funny thing was that I must have thrown out about five grand's worth, just because I can't stand beef-and-tomato-flavour soup . . .'

'You're joking?'

I shook my head.

'If you wrote that in a book nobody would believe you,' said Charlotte.

She walked with me all the way to the river.

'So, are you going to stay in Paris?' she asked.

'I think so, for a while. I've been reunited with my errant father and, much to our surprise, we get on brilliantly. And I really like François.'

'François?'

'My father's lover. Yeah, it was a bit of a shock to me, too, at first. My father says he has always known he was bisexual, apparently, and he thinks that was why he could never really sustain a committed relationship with a woman . . . It's funny, I came here expecting a kind of elderly romance, like Sartre and de Beauvoir. I end up staying in La Cage aux Folles.'

We embraced like old friends, then she strolled off back to the library.

*

I started walking across the bridge towards my father's attic on the Ile St-Louis. It was getting colder and a fog was coming down. The floodlights made a smudgy halo around Notre-Dame. It looked too much like a Monet to be real. I pulled my duffle coat tightly around me. I was going to be late for dinner.